# Saying It Straight

*Clark Sturges teaches English
at Diablo Valley College
in Pleasant Hill, California.
His other books are*
A Strategy for Writing *and* Witnesses.

# Saying It Straight

*Writing by Ordinary People*

*Edited by*
*Clark Sturges*

**DMB**
DEVIL MOUNTAIN BOOKS
WALNUT CREEK, CALIFORNIA

*Clark Sturges*

Saying It Straight

©1984 BY CLARK STURGES. DEVIL MOUNTAIN BOOKS, P.O. BOX 4115, WALNUT CREEK, CA 94596. ALL RIGHTS RESERVED.

No part of this work may be reproduced or used in any form or by any means—graphic, electronic, or mechanical, including photocopying, recording, taping, or information and retrieval systems—without written permission from the publisher. Manufactured in the United States of America.

*Design: Wayne Gallup*
*Production: Jazelle Lieske*

LIBRARY OF CONGRESS CATALOG CARD NUMBER: 83-073469
ISBN: 0-915685-01-9

4 5 6 7 · 5 4 3 2 1

# Acknowledgments

ADAMS, J.: "ODYSSEY OF A HERETIC" BY JOE KENNEDY ADAMS. ©1974 BY JOE KENNEDY ADAMS. REPRINTED BY PERMISSION OF THE AUTHOR. FIRST PUBLISHED IN *Madness Network News*.

ADAMS, M.:"LOVE BEHIND GLASS, ONE DOLLAR" BY MARIANNE ADAMS. ©1982 BY THE *Village Voice*. REPRINTED BY PERMISSION OF THE *Village Voice*.

AMBLER: "MAKING A DIFFERENCE" BY BONNIE AMBLER. ©1982 BY BONNIE AMBLER. REPRINTED BY PERMISSION OF THE AUTHOR. FIRST PUBLISHED BY *The Los Angeles Times*.

BIFFLE: "OF POETRY, DUST AND DEATH" BY CHRISTOPHER BIFFLE. REPRINTED WITH PERMISSION FROM CALIFORNIA LIVING MAGAZINE OF THE SAN FRANCISCO SUNDAY EXAMINER & CHRONICLE, COPYRIGHT ©1975, *San Francisco Examiner*.

BOE: "GRANDMA BEELY AND THE SHOE STORE SIT-IN" BY JOHN BOE. ©1982 BY JOHN BOE. REPRINTED BY PERMISSION OF THE AUTHOR. FIRST PUBLISHED IN *Across the Generations*.

BONGARTZ: "CONFESSIONS OF AN EX-NEWSBOY" BY ROY BONGARTZ. COPYRIGHT ©1975 BY *Harper's Weekly*. ALL RIGHTS RESERVED. REPRINTED FROM THE FEB. 21, 1975 ISSUE BY SPECIAL PERMISSION.

CHIARRELLO: "SICK AT HEART" BY SUSAN CHIARRELLO. ©1983 BY SUSAN CHIARRELLO. REPRINTED BY PERMISSION OF THE AUTHOR. FIRST PUBLISHED BY *California* MAGAZINE, FEBRUARY 1983.

DATAN: "SILENT THUNDER IN THE BRAIN" BY NANCY DATAN. COPYRIGHT ©1975 BY *Harper's Weekly*. ALL RIGHTS RESERVED. REPRINTED FROM THE MAY 9, 1975 ISSUE BY SPECIAL PERMISSION.

FINNEGAN: "GRASS HUTS UP CLOSE" BY BILL FINNEGAN. ©1981 BY BILL FINNEGAN. REPRINTED BY PERMISSION OF THE AUTHOR. FIRST PUBLISHED IN *California* MAGAZINE, DECEMBER 1981.

FRISH: "PLEASE SIGN OFF. YOU'RE FIRED" BY DR. FRISH. ©1983 BY DR. FRISH. REPRINTED BY PERMISSION OF THE AUTHOR. FIRST PUBLISHED BY *The San Francisco Chronicle*.

GRAHAM: "A LITTLE BOY'S PONY" BY BOBBY GRAHAM. BY PERMISSION OF THE AUTHOR'S PERSONAL REPRESENTATIVE.

HILL: "JUST ASKING" BY STEPHANIE HILL. ©1981 BY THE *Village Voice*. REPRINTED BY PERMISSION OF THE *Village Voice*.

LAB: "LOCKED-UP FEELINGS BEHIND BARS" BY LOUIS LAB. ©1982 BY LOUIS LAB. REPRINTED BY PERMISSION OF THE AUTHOR. FIRST PUBLISHED BY *The San Francisco Chronicle*.

Lee: "Verdict for a Bathtub Killing: A Juror's Testimony" by Barbara Lee. Copyright ©1975 by *Harper's Weekly*. All rights reserved. Reprinted from the August 22, 1975 issue by special permission.

Lewis: "A Sunday Afternoon of Blood and Pain" by George H. Lewis. Reprinted with permission from California Living Magazine of the San Francisco Sunday Examiner & Chronicle, Copyright © 1981, *San Francisco Examiner*.

Mooney: "Rescue in the South China Sea" by John Mooney. © 1982 by *The Post-Crescent* (Appleton, WI). Reprinted by permission.

Mundis: "Getting to Headcheese: City People Butcher Their First Pig" by Jerrold Mundis. Copyright ©1975 by *Harper's Weekly*. All rights reserved. Reprinted from the May 23, 1975 issue by special permission.

Rogers: "City Streets: Three Stories from a Policeman's Notebook" by Bob Rogers. Reprinted with permission from California Living Magazine of the San Francisco Sunday Examiner & Chronicle, Copyright © 1982, *San Francisco Examiner*.

Rose: "Gridlock" by Mark Rose. © 1981 by the *Village Voice*. Reprinted by permission of the *Village Voice*.

Schell: "Unexpected Companions in the African Rain Forest" by Tim Schell. This article is reprinted courtesy of *Sports Illustrated* from the April 11, 1983 issue. © 1983 Time Inc.

Silverman: "On Losing a Neighbor" by Arlene Silverman. Reprinted with permission from California Living Magazine of the San Francisco Sunday Examiner & Chronicle, Copyright ©1978, *San Francisco Examiner*.

Sutton: "A Hiss in the Cellar" by William J. Sutton. This article is reprinted courtesy of *Sports Illustrated* from the November 2, 1981 issue. ©1981 Time Inc.

Trownsell: "Higher Education" by Lauren Trownsell. © 1981 by the *Village Voice*. Reprinted by permission of the *Village Voice*.

Vincent: "The First Cadaver is the Worst Cadaver" by Lawrence Vincent. Copyright © 1975 by *Harper's Weekly*. All rights reserved. Reprinted from the March 14, 1975 issue by special permission.

Wyss: "A Surfer's Painful Adventure in Mexico" by Dennis Wyss. © 1983 by Dennis Wyss. Reprinted by permission of the author. First published by *The San Francisco Chronicle*.

Yee: "The Passing of My Confucian Father" by Richard Yee. Reprinted with permission from California Living Magazine of the San Francisco Sunday Examiner & Chronicle, Copyright ©1983, *San Francisco Examiner*.

# Preface

This book of twenty-six nonfiction stories is intended for general readers, who, I believe, will be struck by the authenticity conveyed by this writing. The words on these pages speak to us clearly, directly, and honestly because we're being told of an experience—sometimes immediate, sometimes reminiscent—that heightened the writer's awareness in some way. Sometimes the result is humor or irony, sometimes sorrow or anger or even terror.

These stories, unlike most that reach print, were not written by professionals but by people who didn't think of themselves as writers, didn't support themselves by writing, and had jobs far removed from journalism—bartender, nurse, teacher, railroad brakeman, just to name a few.

The selections here were almost all published in newspaper Sunday supplements, "People" sections, Op-Ed pages, or magazines featuring first-person columns. Their settings range from New York, Colorado, and California, to Mexico, Africa, and the Indian Ocean.

Putting words down on paper for others to read isn't easy—it takes time and a willingness to take risks. Most of us are willing to settle for talk. Speech is fleeting and we know we won't be held accountable for our ramblings, interruptions, redirections, "uhs," and "you knows" (unless someone has a hidden tape machine!). Writing, on the other hand, seems permanent, and we're often reluctant—in fact, sometimes scared—to set down anything tentative or doubtful. But to use writing to make sense of the world around us, to give order and understanding to it, we have to take these risks, as do the authors in this book.

Richard Yee tells us in beautiful and moving detail his father's traditional ways ("The Passing of My Confucian Father"). Bonnie Ambler introduces us to thirteen-year-old Shannon, a friend of her daughter's, and tells us what Shannon taught her ("Making a Difference"). Bob Rogers takes us on his beat in San Francisco ("City Streets: Three Stories from a Policeman's Notebook"). Lauren Trownsell describes the twelve-year-old boys who run numbers out of her New York bar ("Higher Education"). Bobby Graham chronicles the time she and her husband owned a race horse ("A Little Boy's Pony"). And this is just a sampling—the other twenty-one stories are equally varied and powerful.

While only a few of us have the interest and commitment to support ourselves by writing, many of us have the ability to write well when the occasion arises, as this collection illustrates. Good writing—clear, direct, and authentic—is not an exclusive province of professionals; it is within reach of everyone who uses writing to give shape and meaning to experience.

*Clark Sturges*

## Contents

| | |
|---|---:|
| **A Hiss in the Cellar**/ *William J. Sutton* | 1 |
| **A Surfer's Painful Adventure in Mexico**/ *Dennis Wyss* | 10 |
| **Making a Difference**/ *Bonnie Ambler* | 15 |
| **The Passing of My Confucian Father**/ *Richard Yee* | 18 |
| **Confessions of an Ex-Newsboy**/ *Roy Bongartz* | 26 |
| **Gridlock**/ *Mark Rose* | 33 |
| **Unexpected Companions in the African Rain Forest**/ *Tim Schell* | 38 |
| **Grass Huts Up Close**/ *Bill Finnegan* | 41 |
| **Odyssey of a Heretic**/ *Joe Kennedy Adams* | 45 |
| **Locked-Up Feelings Behind Bars**/ *Louis Lab* | 51 |
| **Love Behind Glass, One Dollar**/ *Marianne Adams* | 57 |
| **Please Sign Off. You're Fired!**/ *Dr. Frish* | 60 |
| **The First Cadaver is the Worst Cadaver**/ *Lawrence Vincent* | 67 |
| **Sick at Heart**/ *Susan Chiarrello* | 70 |

| | |
|---|---|
| A Sunday Afternoon of Blood and Pain/ *George H. Lewis* | 76 |
| Higher Education/ *Lauren Trownsell* | 80 |
| City Streets: Three Stories from a Policeman's Notebook/ *Bob Rogers* | 84 |
| Verdict for a Bathtub Killing: A Juror's Testimony/ *Barbara Lee* | 90 |
| Rescue in the South China Sea/ *John Mooney* | 96 |
| A Little Boy's Pony/ *Bobby Graham* | 99 |
| Just Asking/ *Stephanie Hill* | 104 |
| On Losing a Neighbor/ *Arlene Silverman* | 107 |
| Getting to Headcheese: City People Butcher Their First Pig/ *Jerrold Mundis* | 112 |
| Of Poetry, Dust and Death/ *Christopher Biffle* | 119 |
| Silent Thunder in the Brain/ *Nancy Datan* | 129 |
| Grandma Beely and the Shoe Store Sit-In/ *John Boe* | 136 |

# Saying It Straight

# A Hiss in the Cellar

by *William J. Sutton*

We're lost when we leave our cities. Those of us born and raised there don't know how to function when we find ourselves in the "natural" world that's so large and strange to us. Things aren't made to our scale out there. The space seems limitless. Rules apply there that man didn't make, and they aren't written; they're learned from experience. That's sometimes a painful experience—sometimes a lethal one.

I learned that shortly after moving in midwinter to a town in Colorado named Parker, about 25 miles southeast of Denver. My wife and I were going to try to breed and raise thoroughbred horses, while I worked as a supervisor in a catalogue house to help make ends meet. So we leased a little spread, with a modest house, a barn and a quarter section of land. A quarter section is 160 acres, which, if it were in a square parcel, would measure a half mile on a side. It was, to me, a lot of land.

The surprises that nature gave us were pleasant at first: Watching a herd of mule deer move slowly up a draw at the bottom of the hill my house was on with the does in the lead. Seeing an owl fly like a giant butterfly through a silent, snow-spangled night. Listening to the coyotes bicker at 5 a.m. over something they had caught. Heading for the barn one morning and finding a herd of antelope grazing in the pasture. I felt as though I had returned to Eden and was a new Adam, naming the animals as I found them. I thought it was fun.

Around St. Patrick's Day, we had a spell of weather that was sweet and warm beyond believing. As I would find out later, Denver doesn't really have a spring as I knew it, but this was a beautiful and premature imitation. We took advantage of it by saddling up and going for a nice ride.

---

*William J. Sutton now lives in New Haven, Connecticut, where he is a sales-training manager for General Electric.*

The first thing I noticed when we got back to the house was a very loud, high-pitched noise. It sounded like gas or steam escaping under pressure. It seemed to be coming from the basement. I opened the outside door to the cellar. We had two dogs, which we kept in the basement whenever we'd leave. Normally, they would tumble out of the doorway as soon as it was opened. They didn't. They stuck their heads around the corner at the bottom and then retreated out of sight.

I started down the cellar stairs, mentally tabulating what it was going to cost to get someone this far out into the country to fix a broken line. My suspicions about the cause of the sibilant noise were rapidly approaching confirmation as I reached the bottom of the steps. I'd pinpointed the sound as coming from the water heater, but as I turned toward the heater, I didn't see any escaping steam or water. The dogs came up to me excitedly, and then ran back toward the water heater, and in that instant I saw what was making the sound.

There on the floor next to the heater was a prairie rattlesnake, coiled and rattling, ready to strike. The dogs seemed all set to go for him when I yelled for them to stay. I don't know if I'd ever yelled that loud before in my life. They backed off and I chased them up the stairs. Adam had a new animal to name. It wasn't as much fun as before.

I ran back upstairs and slammed the door shut as though the snake were coming up the stairs. "There's a damn rattlesnake down there," I said to my wife. Then, as if someone had given me instructions, I headed for the barn.

"Where are you going?" she asked me.

"To get a hoe."

I could have tried shooting the snake, but I realized that a stray bullet offered all kinds of potential hazards. The snake was more or less in a corner and a rifle shot could ricochet off a wall with dire effect to the water heater or even myself. I would somehow have to kill the snake without shooting it, and the hoe seemed like my best bet.

A phrase came to mind that we'd used in the service to describe a crisis situation: gut check. At the time this was happening, though, I didn't consider it to be a test of courage. I only wanted it to be over.

Hoe in hand, I reopened the basement door with dread. The noise was still going on. As I went downstairs all kinds of doubts went through my mind. I was about to attempt something that was totally outside my experience. Nothing had ever happened in my life to prepare me for a moment like this. I had no idea if I would succeed, but I had to. As far as I knew, the only way to get the snake out of the basement was for me to kill it and take it out. I reached the bottom of the stairs hoping it was all a bad dream, and the snake wouldn't be there. He was there. At that moment I was filled with an overwhelming wish to be somewhere else, anywhere else. If sheer mental effort could transport a man, I'd have been gone.

I raised the hoe and slowly moved toward the snake. I had to kill it, but I didn't know how to begin. I could see its eyes watching me, and behind its head a blur, which was its tail. The sound was indescribable, echoing off the concrete, like the chirr of locusts on a summer night.

I pushed the hoe in its face, tentatively, the way a boxer jabs at an opponent in the early rounds to measure him. I didn't know what the hell I was doing; I just felt that I had to do something. The snake wasn't impressed. It struck at the hoe. Successfully. As I pulled it back I could see the venom dripping down the blade.

At that instant of fumbling and frustration, the training of forgotten years suddenly paid off. In desperation, my brain went back to boot camp—Marine Corps Recruit Depot, San Diego. I recalled fighting with pugil sticks at bayonet practice. I hadn't distinguished myself at that activity, but I had new motivation. I struck a stance that was probably ridiculous, but who was watching? I raised the hoe overhead and brought it down in the middle of the snake. At the same time, I let out a yell that would've made a drill instructor proud. The hoe connected somewhere in the snake's midsection. It stretched out from its coiled position, and I yelled and struck again. I think at this time I was reacting as much from fear as anything else. I don't know how many more times I hit it. When I was done it was dead.

I felt triumphant. I was victorious, not so much over the snake as over circumstances that only moments before had overwhelmed me. But even in my euphoria, I found it odd that the noise persisted, seemingly as loud as before. As I went back upstairs I vaguely recalled an old wives' tale about rattlesnakes—after you kill one its tail keeps going until sundown. It didn't make sense, but I was new to such mysteries. I informed my wife of the demise of our guest. I think I probably swaggered a bit as I headed toward the barn to put the hoe away.

Before I got there, I met Dean, my landlord, standing at the pasture gate. "Dean," I said, "how long does it take for a rattlesnake's tail to stop going after he's dead?"

"Why, did you kill one?"

"Yup."

"Where?"

"In the basement."

*"In the basement!"*

"Yup."

"Let's go."

And we went. We heard the sound as soon as we got back to the house. "I don't understand it. I'm sure it's dead," I said. Down the stairs again, and around the corner. The corpse was still there, motionless. The sound was still being made. We walked up to the dead snake.

I don't know which of us saw the other rattlesnake first. It was about three feet from us, in the corner, coiled between the wall and a vertical two-by-six. It was actually off the ground, wrapped into that space like a pretzel.

Dean swore and grabbed the hoe from me. The blade was too wide to fit into the space, so he turned the hoe around and used the handle to poke at the snake, trying to scrape it out of there. The snake writhed and twisted. If you have ever seen a snake move, you have some appreciation for the strange feeling that its motion generates in the watcher. The nature of the snake's musculature or something gives the impression that the snake is going in different directions at the same time. It gives you an eerie feeling. It doesn't seem possible that you're watching one creature go through all that motion. Dean got the snake to move out onto the floor and gave it one good whack behind the head amd killed it. At last the basement was quiet. We got a paper bag and a shovel and scooped the two snakes into the bag. And then we went upstairs and had a drink.

As we drank, we tried to figure what my wife and I should do next. Circumstances prevented impulsive action. It just isn't possible to move 20 head of horses on the spur of the moment. We had no idea how the snakes had got in there. We had no idea if there were others or if there would be others. We eventually persuaded ourselves that the warm weather had caused these two snakes to come out of their hibernation earlier than usual, that they somehow got into our basement, and that it was a one-time occurrence.

Later that night I went into the basement to test our one-time theory and put my mind at rest. I took a flashlight to be thorough. I even went so far as to shine the light along the tops of the walls, where the beams supporting the floors above rested, and when I saw the pattern of a six-inch section of snake slowly moving above my head, I couldn't believe it. My breath stopped. I moved the light away and then back again. The snake was still there. I went back upstairs. Once again, I didn't quite know what to do next. My wife, by now, was nearly hysterical. She wanted to leave and check into a motel. I didn't see that we were in any immediate danger—but that was a long night.

I went to work the next day and had a good time telling the story. My enjoyment was much less intense that night when I returned home, checked the basement and found the snake again. It was in a different location, but it was there. And I had to figure out how to get rid of it.

I decided to shoot it with my 20-gauge. I couldn't think of any alternative. It was located above my head, I could see only a small section of its body, I didn't know where its head was, and I couldn't see any wires or pipes around it.

I told my wife to keep the dogs out of the part of the house above where I was going to shoot and to stay away herself, in the unlikely event that the pellets penetrated the floor. And I shot it. It writhed and I shot it again. It fell from the ledge and scared me nearly dead, but it was the one that was dead.

After that, assuming there were more snakes in the cellar, we settled down to a siege. We couldn't just pull up and leave because the horses couldn't be abandoned. We weren't really in any danger because the snakes couldn't get into our living quarters—and we didn't go into the basement unnecessarily, believe me. The siege even had certain advantages: On a slow

Saturday, I could always grab a weapon and go down to the basement to hunt snakes. And I kept finding them, one at a time.

We called county agents, zoos, exterminators, and fish and game agencies looking for a way to get rid of them en masse. And we got suggestions. It's truly amazing how people will feel obligated to answer a question, even when they don't have an answer. We were advised to buy a mongoose and turn it loose. Someone else said to get a pig, that it could combat rattlers with immunity because of its protective fat. One of the more imaginative answers had a certain appeal—it was to put out saucers of Black Flag and let the snakes eat it. The appeal was that it sounded so simple. Another theory was to get some bull snakes and put them in the basement with the rattlers. Somehow the bull snakes would engage the rattlers in combat and emerge victorious. Well, I'm pretty gullible, but before acting on advice that seemed less than profound, I thought I'd turn to my ace in the hole. My ace in the hole, my sure thing, was my friend, Lloyd Goding, who was about to get a master's degree in biochemistry at the University of New Mexico. His field of study was in warfirins, which are kinds of rodent poison. Would he know how to get rid of these snakes? Does a koala bear like eucalyptus? I mean this was solid.

I related the whole business to Lloyd, complete with all the flaky suggestions. He took it all in, said he wanted to talk to the dean of his department, who was a herpetologist, and then he'd call me back. To his credit, I don't think he laughed. Three hours later the phone rang. "Hello," I said.

"Let me tell you exactly what he said," Lloyd said. "Are you ready?"

"Yes."

"Use a gun or a club. And be very careful when you pick them up, because the venom is still dangerous."

"That's it? What about . . . ?"

"Forget all the rest. Black Flag is good for cockroaches and other insects, but it won't do much against snakes, particularly since I don't know how you'd get them to eat it."

"Yeah. Thanks."

I can't say I was surprised by Lloyd's bleak report. One final phone call did get an exterminator who said he had a method that he used for Minuteman missile silos—it involved the use of cyanide and would render the house uninhabitable for two years. I didn't think Dean would endorse that idea, although he'd said that he'd told his insurance man about my problem and asked the man's advice. The insurance agent had recommended burning the place down, saying he'd rather have a fire insurance claim on the house than a liability suit resulting from a death from snake bite that had occurred on the property.

Weeks went by, and the battle went on. I tried to lure the rattlers out of hiding and into the center of the basement, feeling it would be easier to kill what was easily seen. This effort involved buying a mouse cage and two mice. I hung the cage from the basement ceiling. No luck. One mouse escaped, and the other died a natural death.

We discovered how the snakes had gotten into the cellar. There was a full basement under only half the house. The other half was just a crawl space. The entrance to the crawl space was a two-by-two boarded opening in the wall behind the water heater. I took the cover off the opening and could see into the crawl space. At the other end I could see a small hole in the foundation. Apparently the snakes had come in through that hole the previous fall. Perhaps they had been attracted to the full basement because it was warmer than the crawl space; they had entered the larger room by dropping over from the top of the wall separating it from the crawl space.

Looking into the crawl space one day, I saw the outline of a large snake. I killed it easily with one shot from the 20-gauge. There were no problems with wires or pipes in the crawl space. But now there was a problem with that snake. It was 25 or 30 feet into an unlighted space that was probably occupied with friends of the deceased. Spring was on the way. Warmer weather not only meant more activity from my tenants, but it also meant the decomposition of the corpse. I had no idea what a rotting snake smelled like. I didn't want to know. Neither did I want to go in there to get it out. This dilemma set up the Last Great Snake Adventure.

It started, as so many things do, with a conversation. Dean was over one Sunday and the talk turned to snakes, as usual. I remarked about the remains in the crawl space and wondered aloud about how to get the dead snake out. If memory serves, we were having tall Scotches at the time. More than one. A look of resolve came onto Dean's face. "Hell, I'll go in there and get it out. You guys have put up with enough. You don't have to smell a dead snake." (I should comment that Dean was generous almost to a fault during this whole debacle.)

We went to the barn and got a 400-watt light. I secured several extension cords. The idea was to give Dean some light to take with him as he wriggled around in the crawl space. He would, at his insistence, go in with my short-barreled .22/410. I was going to "cover him" with my 20-gauge. I held onto that shotgun as moral support. I didn't actually expect any snakes to attempt an ambush.

Looking back, I don't think I really had any understanding of the bravery I was seeing. Dean was going into a space so confining that he couldn't even begin to stand up. He was going to be in darkness except for the narrow beam of light emitted by his hand-held lamp. His only exit would be through an opening that measured about two feet square. And he might be entering a space occupied by dozens of venomous snakes. Maybe we were just fools. Or drunk.

But back into the basement we went. It was beginning to smell like something left over from World War II, what with all the gunfire that had gone on.

As we took the cover off the crawl space, I said, "Are you sure you want to do this?"

"Hell, no. You think I shouldn't?"

"Let's go."

And, light in one hand and gun in the other, Dean crawled through the opening. His back was to me and he was just beginning to turn around when the light went out. You could've heard him yell in Kansas. So many words were coming out of him at once that it was hard to know what he was asking for, but clearly his first priority had to be to get the light fixed. He was screaming for me to find where the connection had broken in the line of extension cords. I frantically fed the cord through my hands, looking for something that wasn't right. I didn't have any luck, but suddenly, with Dean still yelling, the light came back on. Dean said sheepishly, "I stepped on the damn thing and broke a connection up at this end." Then he looked up and said, "There's one right there," and I moved back from the opening as he raised the gun and shot the snake. It was a very small one, less than 12 inches long. We had reached the point of measuring them, almost like fish. We were disappointed by the little ones.

Well, Dean kept crawling around in there and accomplished a lot. He got the corpse of the large snake out. He found and killed a total of seven more rattlers, ranging in size to about 18 inches and bringing to 18 the total that had been found in the house.

Several weeks later, in May, I would discover the 19th and last rattler. It had been weeks since we'd seen any, and we'd just about concluded that we were through with them. Habits are sometimes hard to break, though, and I still patrolled the basement on a regular basis. During one such patrol, on a weekend, I spotted No. 19. It was up in the beams, where the third one I'd killed had been. The pattern of its skin was visible, and the thickness of its body indicated it was another large one. I used the .22 and shot it through the middle of its body. The shock caused it to flip over as it fell right toward me. Almost in a panic, I jumped to avoid the snake. It landed on the cement floor, writhing and rattling, its back broken. I raised the gun, aimed for its head, pulled the trigger and killed it. While my body was doing those things, I was feeling a sadness at the act. The snake wasn't there by choice; instinct had driven it into my house to seek a place to hibernate. It wasn't moved by malice or design to put me and mine in danger. But it *was*, without doubt, dangerous, and it seemed to me that I'd failed because I'd been unable to neutralize that danger without destroying life. I killed it because I had to, and I was sorry that I had to.

We found a place to move to by summer, although no more snakes were left in the crawl space by then, we were certain. Dean said that there was an old Indian belief that if you hung a dead rattler out to dry, it would bring rain. We hung a few on the fence at the end of May. It rained every day in June.

# A Surfer's Painful Adventure in Mexico

*by Dennis Wyss*

The white Mexican sun broiled down as the battered taxi lurched over the mountain road. With every jolt, pain from my dislocated shoulder shot through my body.

Despite the searing heat, I shivered with uncertainty—I had no idea where to find a doctor in the jungle-covered hills or deserted beaches of southern Mexico.

An hour earlier, surfing at a rugged beach called Zipilete, I miscalculated the speed and power of a large, barrel-shaped wave. It ground me into the coral-studded floor of the seabed, wrenching my left arm from its socket.

I was now on my way in search of a doctor, accompanied by my traveling companion, frantic with worry, and an unlikely Samaritan.

Taxis are seldom seen along the 15 miles of unpaved, unshaded and eroded road that runs from the beach and across coastal hills to Puerto Angel, the small fishing village where we were staying. We had walked half a mile up from the beach when a taxi careened around a bend ahead of us.

The driver, a boy in his late teens wearing a blue Dallas Cowboys T-shirt and cracked mirror sunglasses, skidded to a stop. Wide-eyed with fright and fascination, he said he would take us where we wanted to go.

"No doctor Puerto Angel," he said. "Pochutla."

God. Pochutla was another 12 miles inland from Puerto Angel.

Fifteen agonizing miles later, we passed through Puerto Angel. For the next 12 miles of narrow and winding road, the boy put the complaining Datsun through its paces: Speeding

---

*Dennis Wyss is a San Francisco-based student, poet, and traveler who has given up surfing and taken up chess.*

down straightaways and barely letting up on curves, he blared the horn at anything—goats, burros, people—walking along the side of the road.

We skidded into Pochutla, scattering pigs, chickens and grubby youngsters. Stopped at last in front of the doctor's office, the driver announced—with compassion in his eyes as he glanced again at my distended shoulder—that we owed 400 pesos. The trip normally costs 100.

We didn't argue.

The doctor's office, like most of the buildings in Pochutla, was old and weather-beaten. A middle-aged woman sat behind a flimsy wood partition. She smiled. We said, in halting Spanish, that I had hurt my arm. No one came running.

"*Siente se, por favor,*" she said pleasantly.

Obediently, we sat.

And we waited.

The previous summer after I had dislocated the same shoulder, I had been in the emergency room at San Francisco General Hospital only 30 seconds before a nurse shot morphine into my grateful arm.

My companion tried to remain calm. Every now and then, her concentration lapsed: "Where the hell is the doctor? Can't they see you're in pain?"

"It's OK," I said. Hemingway stoicism. Grace under pressure. Lasts about a minute.

An Indian woman in a pink flowered dress and a grizzled old campesino in a straw sombrero were also waiting. For 30 minutes they stared impassively at the bloody, sunburned gringo, hunched over and cursing under his breath.

My arm was getting numb. Great, I thought. If the ball stays out of the socket long enough to injure a nerve, I lose all feeling in the arm.

The door to the doctor's office opened. A voice called my name.

The small office was cluttered with stacks of paper, plaques and medical journals. The doctor was in his mid-30s, dressed in slacks and a sport shirt. Stocky, with a handsome face, slightly drooping eyes and a thick black mustache, he looked tired.

"I only speak a little English," he said, smiling apologetically.

I nodded and tried to grin.

"Where are you from?"

"*Estados Unidos.* San Francisco."

"Ah, *si*, San Francisco, beautiful city, *muy bonito, muy bonito,*" he said. His voice trailed off.

I did not feel conversational.

"*Dislocado.* Have you ever done this before?" he asked.

"Twice," I said, as calmly as I could. I told him I was losing feeling in the lower part of my arm.

He reached out, grabbed and gave it a slight, sharp twist above the elbow.

I jumped. But the feeling returned. In a big way.

The doctor, after looking somewhat askance at my fiercely protective companion, led me to a small, dark room that housed his vintage X-ray machine. He X-rayed the shoulder.

Then, he said, "Have a seat."

He went back to his office and called in the Indian woman. My companion started cursing again.

Twenty minutes later, the Indian woman walked out, and the receptionist motioned for the old man. My companion leaped up from her chair and started pacing wildly: "What kind of doctor is this guy...they're making you wait because we're gringos."

By this time I could no longer sit still. The only way I could possibly deal with the pain was to pace the reception area.

The old man left. We were alone.

The doctor came out of his office and sat down next to me. "I know what is wrong with your arm," he said. "I am going to try and put it back in the...the...*socket* without any anesthetic."

I blanched.

"I can do this," he assured, "only if you can relax the... the...*musskles* in your chest and arm. If you can relax, it won't be hard."

I nodded. All I wanted after having had the arm out for two hours, was to get the thing back in. "OK," I said. "Let's get it on."

"*Pardon?*" he asked. "*No comprende.*"

"*Si, si.* OK," I groaned.

The doctor motioned me up onto a gurney built for people a foot shorter than I. He flicked on a large circular overhead lamp. A young woman walked into the room. This was his wife, he said. She would assist.

She put both arms across my chest to hold me down. The doctor grasped my wrist and elbow and began to straighten the arm.

I practically leaped off the table.

"*Tranquilo,*" the doctor said.

For the next 20 minutes, he worked that arm.

I tried to relax. I tried not to scream. I failed. Miserably.

"*Tranquilo, tranquilo,*" the doctor insisted.

The arm would not go in.

Finally the doctor informed me, apologetically, that he would have to put me under.

"*Si,*" I gasped.

The doctor's wife wheeled in a hanger from which a bottle went into a vein on my good arm. The doctor asked me my age and how much I weighed. After pursing his lips and stroking his mustache for a moment, he spoke a few numbers in rapid Spanish to his wife. She paused, then countered with a few figures of her own.

The lights spun and a numbing warmth crept through me. I heard the doctor chuckle, and I was out.

I came spinning down a long, dark tunnel with a small light at the end. The light got bigger. I was looking at the sad face of an Indian girl who was looking down at me. Then she turned into a ceiling.

I was on my back. My arm was back in the socket, and the arm and shoulder were wrapped firmly in a soft bandage. The needle was still in my arm. After a while I got up, found my huaraches and woozily walked to the door, pulling the hanger and bottle with me.

The doctor saw me and walked over, smiling.

"How do you feel?" he asked.

"*Bien, muy bien,*" I said.

"*Bien.* Let us go X-ray your shoulder to make sure it is correct," he said.

It was.

I thanked the doctor. He nodded, flashed a slight, tired smile and disappeared into his office.

The receptionist began to write up the bill. Despite the lingering glow of morphine, I felt a new rush of anxiety.

The bill at San Francisco General, I suddenly remembered, was $300.

The receptionist handed over the tab. My companion counted out 4800 pesos—$32.

The next day, to show our gratitude, we dropped by the doctor's office with a bottle of brandy. The waiting room was crowded. The doctor was busy and couldn't see us right now, the receptionist said, but he would be out soon.

"*Siente se,*" she said.

# Making a Difference
## *by Bonnie Ambler*

Shannon entered my life through the doorway of the intensive-care unit of Long Beach Memorial Hospital, where my daughter was awaiting surgery for a blood disorder.

Shannon was also a patient and the self-appointed goodwill ambassador of the hospital's children's unit. She had heard that my daughter, Heather, five, was having a hard time with all the pre-surgery tests, tubes and procedures.

"Gee, I'm just a kid, too, and I get needles all the time," Shannon said, showing how she was attached to an I.V. unit on a stand she wheeled along. "They really are rotten, but if they make you better, I guess they're OK." Somehow, hearing this from another child gave Heather the faith and strength to face her ordeal.

I soon discovered that Shannon made regular rounds to most of the children's rooms, relieving fears and bringing bits of joy to each.

One day she told me that, while she couldn't be around large crowds of people and risk infection, she could visit the hospital coffee shop late at night if accompanied by an adult. Since I was living at the hospital during Heather's crisis, I was glad to return this small favor.

The trips to the coffee shop became a great adventure. Around midnight, the nurses seemed to disappear, or at least look the other way as Shannon and I maneuvered wheelchair and I.V. stand into the elevator and through the halls.

In the coffee shop, while consuming startling quantities of pie, Shannon would share with me her thoughts about life, which were deep and far beyond her years. When I was wondering if my daughter would respond to therapy, or even if she would live, it was Shannon who fed me the strength to face

---

*Bonnie Ambler lives in Rancho Palos Verdes, California, and keeps a personal journal of her impressions, from which this story evolved.*

whatever happened. She was quiet and gentle with me in those dark hours, but when Heather did respond it was Shannon who led the celebration.

Shannon was equally open with me about her own feelings and fears. Her disease, aplastic anemia, is a particularly ugly one. The bone marrow fails to produce adequate blood cells, and the subsequent lowered resistance to infection often proves fatal. Most insidiously, it usually attacks teenagers and young adults.

Shannon survived only through continuous blood transfusions. The hope was that her own body would start producing healthy blood. Failing that, she would die.

Shannon's greatest fear about the prospect of death was that it would come before she had lived long enough "to make a difference" in her world.

In addition to making her rounds and writing for the hospital newsletter, she wanted to do something more permanent. With the help of her social worker, she persuaded the hospital to finance a video tape, "Shannon's View," to be shown to health workers and families involved with children stricken by catastrophic illnesses, to help them understand the child's feelings.

After my daughter was released from the hospital, I still went back often for midnight coffee shop "raids," as we called them. By then, Shannon's condition had worsened, and although she was confined to bed she sensed my anxiety and insisted that we talk. It was this night that Shannon spelled out what she called the bottom line: "Are you happy; is your world OK?"

Those words made me step back and really look at my situation: Heather was ill, but she would recover. Everyone else important to me was alive. There was nothing terribly wrong elsewhere in my life. I had to admit that on "the bottom line" it was a special day, one to be thankful for.

I short time later, a mass was discovered in Shannon's chest, and the transfusions to keep her alive were not going well. I marveled that she never lost her smile, her happy outlook or concern for others. Her "rounds" were less frequent, but still she managed to bring a special magic to other children wherever she encountered them. Her world was OK and every day was worth celebrating.

One night, her mother asked if I would sit with Shannon for a while. She radiated a glow and looked more beautiful than ever. I felt a special kind of communication without the need for words. When I left after two hours, I knew then Shannon was leaving too, but for some reason I accepted this.

Shannon Gordon died the next morning in her mother's arms. Her life had lasted 13 years—long enough to make a difference.

# The Passing of My Confucian Father

*by Richard Yee*

When my father died, a "dark cloud of unknowing" hung over me. Neither my own Christian belief that death is the joyous entry into eternal life nor my father's Confucian view that the dead are continually renewed through ancient rites could dissipate that cloud. To have marked his end with Christian optimism would have distorted the meaning of the manner of his living. And yet, for his children, his Confucian verities were not wholly and easily transplanted to American soil. The conflicting and compromised views could not proffer the gut strength to withstand the awesomeness which is death. And so the cloud hovered, dulling the acts of life: Prayers were only murmured, smiles were wan and when my hands opened, they bore no gifts. Compulsively I would light one cigarette after another, as if the dots of amber would burn away the wide, dark cloud. The amber only turned to ashes.

Yet inexorably the sun runs its course and inexplicably the outer edges of the cloud burned away, so that here (not there in the stillness of the unknown) and now (two years later), my father moved as it were into a new life. Now is the time to speak of his dying, when I am no longer struck dumb by it. Now is the time to retrace the Confucian path that he took to his death, before his life is reduced to the silent markings on his tombstone.

The path of my father's dying was a long one: in space, from China to the United States; in time, 88 years. His father had preceded him to America but had left his children in China to insure a Chinese upbringing. Rigidly schooled in the Confucian classics in the dying days of the Qing dynasty—rigid precisely because the dynastic ways were passing—my father

---

*Richard Yee teaches philosophy at Holy Names College in Oakland, California.*

would have preferred remaining in China: He wanted to study Chinese medicine. My grandfather, I am told, crumpled the letter announcing that desire and ground it underfoot. "Lazy, long-gown scholar!" he denounced. And so my father came to work in his father's laundry at Seventh and Howard streets. He joined the many Chinese in San Francisco, each sustaining the other in the dream of returning rich to China to become landed gentry, rich enough to rescue their children from barbaric Western ways.

But World War II came and economic opportunities quite suddenly teased my father's nine children with new dreams. The elder ones experienced the sophistication of being paid by checks instead of wages in small manila envelopes. The younger ones began to croon Top Ten tunes rather than listen to the strident sounds of Chinese opera singers. Most important of all, the language around the dinner table changed to a bewildering hodgepodge of Chinese and English to describe our new world. Eventually Confucian terms like "filial piety" and "the superior man," which resonate with life in Chinese, became flat and dull when uttered in English. My father did not seem to notice.

The Communist victory in China ended his dream of returning, but his retirement granted him leisure to shore up his idea of a perfect world: to concoct elaborate Chinese dishes, to serve in the Yee Family Association, to read the Chinese daily. Above all, he spent hours composing letters. His letters were always drafted, corrected and then recopied in a calligraphic style that was perhaps too stiff but showed years of learning. For him, calligraphy was a measure of moral character; the movements of the hand flowed from what was practiced in the heart.

Leisure also granted what his father had thwarted. My father read his Chinese medical books, felt his own pulse or that of one of his children, and then wrote out a prescription for herbs. We would be secretly amused; to us it seemed the illness diagnosed was always linked to the particular page he was studying. No doubt our judgment stemmed from our smug preference for the antiseptic efficiency of Western pills over the heady odors of bitter herbs. We had become Westernized. My father's ways seemed quaint and a bit absurd.

After more than 10 years of these leisurely diversions, my father suffered a stroke that left his right side paralyzed. I flew home from school and found him propped up in bed, confident with his patrician expectations, quite enjoying all the attention he judged his due. He would do nothing for himself, not even wash his own face. Within his perfect world, constructed out of filial piety, he turned total dependency into a virtue.

Although years away from home had encouraged in me a reevaluation of my parents' ways and had kindled an admiration of the coherence of the Chinese way, I had also learned to value the American sense of independence and self-reliance. Useless, however, to appeal to that sense, nonexistent in my father, or to point out to him the hardships his demands placed upon my mother. There was only one tack to take. I asked him whether he wouldn't like to write letters again. He emitted a hiss of contempt for my assumed lack of filial piety. But I persisted, promising him that with physical therapy he could learn to write with his left hand. He knitted his eyebrows, then relaxed them and nodded an assent. Soon he was writing again; the left hand caused the horizontal strokes of the characters to be marred by a slant, but the style was still there.

He now also kept a small brown spiral notebook for his study of English vocabulary. He never could construct fluent sentences in English, though; they always sounded like his clipped, terse, classical Chinese phrases. The word he took most care to learn to pronounce was "ungrateful." Over and over he asked me to pronounce it for him. He never quite mastered the "r" and the "l" sounds. I never knew if he found occasion to use the word. Perhaps he used it as an incantation against the day when his children might become ungrateful, forgetting him, forgetting filial piety.

Two years after my father's stroke, my mother suffered one too, suddenly and fatally. "She had no parting words," my father said. For the first and the last time I witnessed his tears.

With my mother gone, the task of keeping my father at home became very difficult, requiring a constant stream of family members and nurses. But his children wanted to keep him the head of his own house, where large portraits of his parents and now my mother stared down at us, ordering the comings and goings of the household. By means of offerings of incense and food and wine, they participated in the gaiety of all the Chinese festivals and duly received reports of happy events such as weddings and births. In this way, time present and time past merged; the living and the dead were united. In the preserve of that vast order, my father's place was ensured.

The continuity and the certitude of that order were able to quiet the pains and to nudge away the isolation that accompanies illness. Years before "handicap access" entered our consciousness and became codified with legal sanctions, my father and his wheelchair went everywhere. He enjoyed his grandchildren pushing him through Chinatown. He enjoyed even more eating at restaurants, never missing a chance to condemn (often) or to praise (seldom) a dish. He was not to be excluded from these communal pleasures, not because "individual rights" ought to be extended to include the handicapped, but because he was the rightful head of a Chinese household. He deemed that his absence would diminish an occasion, that his presence was a duty. All privileges were grounded in that confidence, never diminished by being discussed.

And his children didn't discuss it—although at times we harbored some resentment of his blindness to the changes brought on simply because we lived in America. Others saw, but he didn't. Once his doctor told me that Chinese were demanding with increasing frequency that he sign papers to commit their parents to nursing homes. The doctor was disheartened and said he feared that possibility each time I telephoned him to check my father's blood pressure. Shrugging my shoulders, I pointed to a sign—a gift from one of his grandchildren—that my father had propped up on the mantel behind his wheelchair. The sign read "King of the House." An ungraceful translation of "filial piety," but it was the best compromise between Chinese sentiments and American perceptions his grandchild was capable of.

An opportunity for a more convenient arrangement, however, did arise. A fellow teacher wanted to sell his house, close to Holy Names College where I teach. I asked my father if he would leave his house and move in with me. "Up to you," was his curt reply. Not a very enthusiastic answer and slightly accusatory. But measured against the difficulty of keeping him in his own house, I took his answer to be sufficient. Just before the purchase was to be made, he spoke to me again. His eyes were lowered to avoid mine, and he shaped his words with care. He did not think moving was a good idea. "Let me explain," he said. "When I die..." Impatient, I wanted to interrupt to say that he had spoken those words too many times during these 10 years since his stroke, but his tone was moderate, wishing neither to command nor to beg, that I held my tongue. "When I die, our relatives will come to pay their last respects. Should I die in your house, they will be coming to your house, not mine." His remarks were not prompted by superstitious visions of his ghost tarrying over familial grounds: His Confucianism kept at bay all ghosts. Nor were they prompted by sentimentality: The decorum of Confucian rites constricted emotional excess.

Rather, my father's position stemmed from the absolute primacy a Confucian confers upon the civilizing experience of the relation between parent and children, an experience that is then extended as a model for all other relations, human as well as spiritual. This alone is the very "way of heaven." The home is a ground hallowed by the labor of parents and laughter of children, making it a fit place to remember ancestors. Only then can a home become a proper place for the councils of cousins and the conviviality of friends. The journey through life follows that progression, otherwise the journey would be a lonely and desolate one. The home where all these relations have been enacted is the only fitting place for a final farewell to a life ordered by these visions, making the home not a castle but a temple. My father's view was not mine, but such clarity of vision merited respect and compliance. And so he remained in his house.

But the clarity of vision from tradition is one thing, the personal process of interiorization of that clarity another. Sometimes unexpectedly a moment sent forth a spark, intensifying the luminosity, speeding the process, both for my father and for me. About a year before my father died, I was making a trip to Reno and asked him if he wanted me to play a few games of keno for him. For the Chinese, keno is not a game of numbers but a game of words. Its 80 numbers count the first 80 words of a 1000-word essay laying out the order of the universe. When he plays the game, a Chinese tries to choose words expressing a sentiment, poetically linking individual fortune to cosmic order. In the past my father had been particularly lucky with words celebrating his union with my mother. But this time he said those words were no longer fitting. Without comment he handed me three new words: "heaven," "earth," "spirit." I too made no comment. I left him alone in his thoughts of his final merging with the larger cosmic order.

Measured against the 17 long years after his stroke, the end, when it came, came quickly. A lingering infection in his paralyzed right foot turned into gangrene. His body revolted: He lost his usual epicurean appetite; his hair became streaked with silver; his bodily functions refused to be controlled. Unlike before, he gave no voice to these assaults upon his body. Only a wincing face from time to time registered the trails of pain that shot through his limbs. His toes darkened and then were slowly eaten away. When the visiting nurse or I dressed the wounds, he averted his eyes and said nothing.

Amputation of his right leg was the only hope against the spread of gangrene. It was a nurse, a gentle woman who spoke Chinese, who made clear the alternative. His answer came in a whisper. At dinner I quietly spoke to him again. He repeated what he had said to the nurse. "I am old..." He faltered, paused to gather strength and lowered his eyes. "I hope it will be quick." He must have practiced that sentence over and over again in his heart. And what is proposed and practiced therein need not be uttered loudly.

"The superior man," Confucious counseled, "will name only what can be described in speech and say only what can be carried out in practice." Death has no name, nor can it be subjected to willful practice; my father left it in silence. He was saying yes to death, yes to the supreme negation. That yes and that no meet only as a contradiction. The truth in that contradiction can be voiced only in silence.

With language diminished during the final days, his eyes seemed to grow in size, protruding and gleaming. They were like the eyes of a cat suddenly tossed into unfamiliar territory: concentrated, alert, watchful. What lay before and what lay behind those eyes never found a voice.

He would have remained at home to keep his vigil, but his

doctor thought some tests in the hospital necessary. The attempts at testing were unsuccessful. "Going home yet?" he uttered over and over. The voice was thin and brittle. His final sentence he addressed to me. "I've taken you away from your work." Years were summed up in that sentence. Was it an apology? Could he have said anything else? He had lived his life in the way he had been taught. More words would have been in vain. Each limited by disparate experiences, we could only part on the compromised shores of human finiteness. So finally he yielded to the ultimate human finiteness of death.

At the funeral services a friend of mine, Kenneth Weisinger, read a poem. Uncannily, my friend had composed the poem at precisely the moment when my father entered a coma.

## *Remembering Mr. Yee*

*Dreaming now of banquets*
   *never tasted,*
*of acres never tilled,*
*looking back at mountains*
*receding not yet vanished—*

*he holds a paper bag*
*filled with candy wrapped in paper*
*to give to children*
*should any come to visit.*

*"Yet it was not for nothing*
*that we came so far from home—*
*here too fields are green*
*and forests cling to cloud,*
   *temples can be built,*
*and if they serve but one*
*generation of man,*
*still there is no loss."*

*Luminous now*
*the gathering clouds*
*he sees them*
*rushing toward him.*

I cannot say I agree with its optimistic conclusions. However, the reference to banquets certainly rang true.

Nothing pleased my father more than a wedding banquet, where older generations greeted the promise of future ones. I recall one he and I attended the summer before his death. His wheelchair was an obvious sign of the effort necessary to show his esteem for the occasion. He was much welcomed by his cousins, who seemed to have formed a line longer than the one to congratulate the bride and groom. In my father's mind the two separate lines merged into one cosmic verity.

I was the speaker at the banquet, having been asked because I spoke both English and the formal Chinese expected at such occasions. After I spoke and returned to my seat, separated from my father's place by the arc of the round banquet table, five or six cousins came to congratulate him. "Uncle Po Chung"—the use of the title distanced him with rank and the use of his name closed the rank in intimacy—"you have done well. Your son knows both Chinese and English." Neither my cousins nor my father said a word to me. The praise was for him alone. And that was right.

# Confessions of an Ex-Newsboy
## by Roy Bongartz

I am about to walk over my old paper route again, on a bright, hot, sunny June afternoon, just 30 years after I quit that business to go off to college. There is an odd clashing in my mind doing this, because there are going to be two paper routes representing themselves as being the real one—the route that has lain more or less dormant in my head all these years, to be traveled only on occasional sleepless nights as one might count sheep, and these real, palpable streets and sidewalks and houses and trees that almost, but not quite, fit the earlier pattern.

There is nothing so portentous as Thomas Wolfe trying to find his soul in Asheville, or Henry Miller skulking around in his old backyard in California, spying on his parents through the kitchen window after years of absence, because my family has long since moved away from Oakwood, the Dayton suburb where we lived and where I had my route. Oakwood is one of those autonomous communities where the moneymakers of certain industrial cities hide out from the real city below. Oakwood remains entirely residential, with no blacks, and but few decorative Jews, among the marvelously complacent Wasp populace. The cops, who were required only to set up speed traps on Far Hills Avenue, to shine flashlights into the parked cars of necking high-school couples at night and to round up Halloween terrorists, all drove *Oldsmobiles*, for Christ's sake.

I am in fact starting out, as I always did after school, from my house at 54 Beverly Place. All the houses seem to be exactly where I left them 30 years ago, all neatly kept up behind their trim gardens and lawns; nothing has been torn down, nothing added. The children—my classmates—who have gradually

---

*This story is from* Harper's Weekly, *published from late 1974 to early 1976, which featured reader-written articles. At that time Roy Bongartz lived in Foster, Rhode Island. Neither* Harper's Magazine *nor this editor knows where he is today.*

inherited the place from their parents have not messed around with Oakwood. But memories do not exactly flood my mind as I walk uneasily down Beverly Place past my house, because this slight shock of strangely combined recognition and non-recognition jars the old life here and makes it seem alien to this new, entirely separate reality. Two men are actually sawing down a big diseased elm tree in front of my house with a chain saw as I come by—in a way it is too good to be true, symbolically marking my return in this theatrical way, but truthfully the tree now has nothing whatever to do with me, and I wonder, did we used to have a big tree in front of the house? We must have.

There is an effect of some kind that pushes me on past, making me want to run away, but I cross the street and walk back down the sidewalk and forcibly slow my steps and inspect the tan brick and the leaded windows of the square, solid-looking, two-story-with-attic house that appears vaguely to be imitating some style that is English. I glance up at an attic window, beyond which I once ran a play radio station and, by wiring our telephone into my Recordio, temporarily short-circuited the entire WAlnut exchange.

The branch office of the *Herald* was only two blocks from my house, in the basement of the Oakwood Pharmacy, on Park Avenue, where a small grocery store, a bakery, and a dry cleaner's made up a circumspect commercial group next to the fire station and police office. The pharmacy used to have a soda fountain all along one side of it and a dark, oiled floor of narrow planks. Before starting out on their routes the newsboys would meet in here—like a bunch of hardhat riveters drinking beer in a Blarney Stone on New York's Sixth Avenue—for great glass mugs of phosphate (fruit-flavored soda with a squirt of phosphoric acid for tang). Now as I walk up Park Avenue, the drugstore presents a baleful facade in opaque concrete, and the door is made of smoked glass, like the windows of a Greyhound bus. Inside there are only rows of closely ranged shelves of patent medicines and beauty aids, and a sign on a stand: *Kosmetic Klearance*. I go around to the alley in back. The *Herald* has been out of business for years, and I resist the faint impulse to go down to the cellar door and try to peer in through the dusty window to see what may be left of the old branch office, scene of daily horseplay and other mild, childish rioting at paper time, stage for a couple of fairly grown-up-type newsboys' strikes, and banquet hall for our annual Christmas turkey dinner (with decorated placemats set out on the wooden benches we used for folding the papers).

Bundles of the final edition, with the front and back pages of the first section printed on deep green newsprint, would arrive around five o'clock every afternoon, and on days when they were a little late—on Thursdays and Fridays when thick papers of 60 and 70 pages would make for a slower press run downtown—the electricity inside the newsboys would begin to spark more nervously, minute by minute, causing alley fights with rolled-up old papers as weapons, or battles with the boys who carried the *Dayton Daily News* from their branch in a garage down a neighboring alley (we would steal and kidnap bundles of the *News* right off their truck, and they would return, later, to sabotage us). Finally the papers would come, delivered in a dark blue Ford van with billboards sporting Hitler headlines on its sides, and the kids would carry in the bundles, usually hiding one of them in the garbage upstairs behind the drugstore in order to enrage their boss, the branch manager, a high-school senior old before his time. Then we would all scream at once for our papers to be counted out.

Now I walk around to the front of the drugstore again. A boy on a bike with a *News* bag full of papers in his wire basket pedals by, and I ask him where the branch is, but they're using individual drop bundles now, no branch office any more, no daily cataclysm. Across the street there is, by God, the Oakwood Bakery, with, in its windows, small four-inch pies of the kind I once won back in the seventh grade when a teacher offered a pie to whomever made the highest grade average during one particular month. Next door, in an ice cream store, I ask for a phosphate, and they still have them too—the real thing, in spite of a price increase from a nickel to 35 cents. No newsboys are lounging in here, though—just teen-aged girls.

I look doubtfully down Park to the corner of Harmon Avenue, where the house of the first customer on my route is waiting for me. It's past five, time for the people to get their papers. I have no bike, no orange *Herald* bag stuffed to bursting with folded papers, and I am older and have put on weight, and I am afraid to go back onto my route. I am worried about taking the short cuts through the back yards, worried about certain dogs—a mangy-mouthed airedale, a pair of uncivilized beagles—who used to chase me, and who eventually bit me. But after 30 years they must be dead, no? This is, after all, my route, isn't it?

I paid 28 cents a customer for this route, and my 70 customers were on the average the richest in all Dayton and its suburbs. They coughed up over a dollar apiece on Newsboys' Day at the end of the year, and the world's thickest malted replaced the phosphates for several days at the drugstore. I look up the shady street at the ornate mansion called Hawthorne Hill, at 901 Harmon—that was a Sunday-only. Orville Wright was the customer there, but it was his maid who always came to the door to pay, and neither I nor the *News* carrier ever got a close look at him. Now it's a guest house for National Cash Register.

As I stroll along, trying to keep my pace slow and even and not to run—run away, run out of this—I know that the two routes, the remembered one and the one unfolding before me as I walk, will never quite jibe. One, the stilled negative, refuses to fit exactly upon the living picture. They are nevertheless very close to each other in detail; each house is here, each turning, each tree; the trees must be taller but they look the same. Space between customers' houses may have been diminished somehow, but this feeling begins to fade after a while. What does not fade is this certain and disturbing sense of walking in two times at once, and there is an Alice-in-the-mirror intrigue in finding that every corner brings on another familiar vista that ought to have been easily predictable, but was not. There must be people, too, back in your head like that, people altogether forgotten, whom you will never again in your whole life think of, unless you happen to turn a corner like this and see them once more, and then they are instantly reborn for you. I turn the corner, down Dixon Avenue, and peer through the dark screen of the porch where at this time of year the young crippled man sat waiting in his wheelchair for the paper. I would walk the paper up to the door for him, and hand it in, and he would always thank me with great cheerfulness, smiling his thin-jawed smile. I can see him clearly now—he's been gone from my mind all that time—but he isn't in this house anymore.

Now, businesslike, I turn down an alley, mentally heave a paper at the back door of a house facing Far Hills Avenue, and come out into the secluded backwater of Harmon Terrace, a hidden L-shaped little street of elegant brick houses, each with an open concrete porch quite near the sidewalk—excellent for easy shots. Then a long throw to the back door of Frank Howland's house—I do not know who lives in any of these houses now, and I don't see much point in finding out—on the corner of Harmon Terrace and Harmon Avenue. Frank, a classmate, was a star on our football team, but he never got into the newsboy business. I now hike down to Oakwood Avenue, lined with Victorian mansions, the old, slightly uneven bricks in the street gleaming softly in the late afternoon sunlight, and at number 1111 I read James Rambo's name on a mailbox before a chic, modern, low-slung California-looking frame house. Jim Rambo—one of the morning *Journal* boys scorned by the afternoon carriers, early risers who spooked around on pitch-black winter mornings before the first trolleybus started its run, with only lonely milkmen to prove that the world was still operational. The *Journal* boys, who used the *Herald* branch office (the two papers had a single publisher), were famous for getting into the branch manager's desk and tearing up the draw sheets and other records, and for breaking into the coal bin (where the Sunday comics were locked up between their arrival on Thursday and delivery Sunday morning) to scatter the papers all over the cellar office. We *Herald* boys imagined they hadn't much future. But here was Jim Rambo's elaborate house, and no way to deny it.

Then I am looking at the Spanish chateau, which was another Sunday-only, I think, with new eyes. It is a veritable chateau, all right, with rococo ornaments along the railings, and arabesques embossed into the stucco, and Spanish decorative tile, and vines, and wrought-iron lamps at the sides of the entrance archway, and a bricked courtyard—but what is it doing in Ohio? The question never occurred to me at all when I was carrying papers here, but now I can see that most of the big estates in this lower, richer part of my route are fashioned after some foreign model or other—Tudor country houses, half-timbered Normandy farms, German medieval castles.

This part of Oakwood looks like a Disneyland without a sense of humor, and here I pumped my bike up and down these long, sweeping driveways all through my most impressionable years, imagining, no doubt—for lack of any obvious evidence to the contrary—that these houses of the rich constituted the standard of beauty in architecture that we would all strive toward if we could afford it.

Here are the homes of the industrial executives, the factories lying in plain view in the city below, a truly baronial setup. Even on hot summer days there was never anything going on outside these houses that a paper boy could see; rear patios and indoor recreation rooms hid the socializing. Once in a while, on a Friday night when collections kept me late, I would run into a cocktail party, and some customer, or his guest, would engage me in drunken, paternal conversation about my future, and would I like to try a snort? But mostly the ornate, make-believe housefronts gave a closed-up feeling, an austere and polite "Keep Out."

The Dayton Country Club is the outermost point on my seven-mile-long route; this afternoon a stylish mother is playing tennis with her grouchy teen-age boy, using green tennis balls; he is complaining about her inconsistent serve and warning her that he has time for only one more game. The swimming pool is guarded from the view of passersby by a high wooden fence; girls visible on the high diving board disappear among shouts and splashes below. Inside the carpeting is thick; here is the long counter in the lobby where I used to deliver the paper every night, sometimes brushing past people in formal dress going inside to a dinner dance. This afternoon there is nobody at the desk. I walk inside the ballroom, and then sneak into the darkened, empty barroom, its panelled walls gleaming from the small lights illuminating the framed oil paintings. On an adjoining terrace the sweep of the green draws the eye toward the city, and to those sustaining factories down there.

Then I hike up the long, curving hill on Thruston Boulevard, where vast acreages of trimmed and evenly watered lawns flow down to the sidewalk from the great houses above. As I pass a driveway entrance, one of the householders, a sinewy, tanned, gray-haired man with the easygoing glance of somebody completely unworried about chance encounters, a self-confident glance, a moneyed glance, says, quite brightly, "Hello, there," to me as I pass. I return the greeting, and go on, and I've walked all the way up the hill, on Far Hills Avenue, and have finished my route, before I realize he is not one of my customers. Not anymore, he's not. He's my own age, or a year or two older, only. He's one of my schoolmates. He's practically me, myself.

# Gridlock

## by Mark Rose

It was 7:30, approaching theater time, a busy period on the East Side, and there were many people on the street hailing cabs. I spotted a big man on the corner of 69th Street, his arm half-raised. I cut over a lane, put on the flasher, and stopped. He took a long time to get in and when he finally managed to maneuver his prodigious frame in the back seat he just sat there singing in Spanish. I was in no hurry. At this time of the night there's no getting away from the traffic or annoyances. The only way to make it through is to try and relax and ride it out. I waited for a while and then the man said, "Take me to the ballroom on 86th, Amigo. I want to go dancing. You want to go dancing, Amigo?"

"No, I don't think so," I said. "Eighty-sixth and what?"

"I don't know, Amigo. Eighty-sixth. I think Lexington. Maybe Third. You know, the ballroom. We go there. We go dancing, Amigo," he said, and commenced to sing merrily.

I put the meter on and pulled out in time to stay with the lights going up the avenue. The man continued singing in a loud voice. It sounded pretty good. I've had a Hasidic Jew chanting, a Greek playing a violin, a child star from Broadway humming show tunes, a fledgling cabaret act practicing "Old Man River," but I never had a Puerto Rican singing before. It was pleasant for a change. But two blocks up the avenue, when the man stopped singing and started talking, the pleasantness quickly drained away.

"How are you taking me, Amigo? This is not the way. I said the ballroom on 86th."

"This is the way," I said. "Straight up Madison. Then we go east."

"No. You're taking me on the West Side. You can't fool me."

Wonderful, I thought. Just what I need.

---

*Mark Rose is an "unemployed hack" who still lives in New York City.*

"Relax and sing. I'll get you there."
"You dance with me, Amigo?"
"Maybe."

I was on my guard now. After you drive a cab for a while it becomes easy to spot a stiff. When they begin to say irrational things and complain about this and that—the way you're going, the condition of the cab, hell, the potholes in the street for that matter—it means they're looking for an excuse to stiff you on the tip, or, worse, not paying the fare at all. A block later, when once again the singing stopped and the talking began, I knew my initial anxiety was justified.

"I'm no dummy. We should be there. Eighty-sixth on the East Side. Where are we?"

I didn't say anything. Maybe he would shut up. Maybe he would suddenly die and I could roll him and drop his carcass in Central Park.

"You go on the East Side. Not the West Side. You hear?"

"We're going right. Don't give me a hard time," I said.

For a half a block he sang, and then he started in again.

"You can't trick me, Amigo, East Side. East Side."

I tried to contain it. My fingers gripped tighter around the wheel.

"You can't fool me, you hear? I demand you go on the East Side."

In one swift, clean motion I turned the wheel of the cab to the right, weaved between a limo and another cab, and stopped short on the corner of 74th Street. I turned to face the man in the back.

"Shut up, just shut up," I said. "I don't want to hear another word out of you until we get there."

"I jus' want to go the right way," he said.

"We're going right. I don't want to hear another word. Understand."

"I jus'..."

"Not another fucking word."

"Okay, okay. I want to go dancing."

"Nada."

He fell silent. I looked hard at the big man's bloodshot eyes and he saw that I meant business. He acknowledged me with a nod of the head and started singing again. The stale smell of alcohol filled the cab. Fuck it. Hopefully he would be quiet now and pay me when we got there. I turned around and continued up Madison.

Barely a block later he started in again. "We should be there. I'm no fool. East Side, Amigo."

It all came apart. Without bothering to look in the rear-view mirror I accelerated and, nearly clipping the front of a cab in the far lane, pulled to the right and stopped by the curb. I knew what I had to do. I calmly got out of the cab, walked around the front, opened the back passenger side door, and pulled him out by the collar of his coat.

"Give me money," I said.

"Why you get mad? We go dancing, Amigo."

"We not go dancing. Give me money," I said, and pushed him backward with both hands toward the wall of a building.

"Don't get mad."

"Money," I said, and pushed him further back until he was up against the building.

"I have this," the man said, and pulled out a bulky paper bag from his coat pocket. "Here."

I grabbed the bag and looked inside.

"Cat food? You're giving me cat food?"

"I have two cats. Good cats. They could not come tonight."

"You're giving me cat food?"

"No, Amigo. Look." He stuck his hand in the paper bag and pulled out a small plastic container. He held the container up at eye level and stared at it with a dumb, satisfied smile, like it was a priceless treasure. "Shrimp salad," he said.

I snatched the container from his hand, stuffed it in the paper bag, and threw the bag on the ground. Then I smacked him on the chest with the palm of my hand. He stood there weaving from side to side, his back braced against the building, and shook his head. I smacked him on the chest again but he didn't respond. It was almost too easy. Although I had never come to blows with a fare before, at least once a night I felt a terrible need to, and there he was standing in front of me, an inebriated, disoriented, frustrated singer who could fulfill the long-denied catharsis quite easily. But no, he wouldn't even give me that. He wouldn't react, even after the third smack on the chest. I reached behind his left side and felt the top of a bottle in his back pocket. No resistance. Then I reached behind his right side and felt the bulge.

"Give me the wallet," I said.

"Be my friend, Amigo, We go dancing."

"Give me the wallet or I'll break your arm."

Without a word he reached behind his back and after several failed attempts, managed to extract his wallet. I grabbed it and opened it up. Surprisingly, it was full of bills. I held it up and opened it wide in front of his face so he could clearly see what I was doing. I separated the bills and started taking them out, one by one.

"Three for the fare," I said, holding up three singles. I took two more. "And two dollars aggravation charge. Now get in the cab, shut up, and I'll take you to the ballroom."

I handed him the wallet and he put it back in his pocket.

"We go dancing?"

"Sure, we go dancing."

"No reason to get mad, Amigo," he said. He scooped up the paper bag with the cat food and shrimp salad, got in the car, and commenced to sing merrily.

When we reached the corner of 86th Street and Third Avenue he let out a big scream. "There, there, that's it!" he said, pointing to the ballroom. I pulled over to the opposite side of the street, but he didn't get out. He sat there singing. I got out of the cab and opened his door.

"This is it, Amigo, end of the line," I said.

"You come dancing with me?"

"I don't think so."

He slowly got out of the cab, clutching his paper bag.

"For you," he said, thrusting the bag in my hand.

"That's okay. Keep the cat food."

"No. For you." He pulled the small container of shrimp salad out of the bag and handed it to me. "Because I like you."

"Okay."

I took the shrimp salad but he still didn't leave. He leaned against the cab, his hand searching for something in his pocket.

"Let's go," I said.

"Don't know," he said with a befuddled look as he patted his coat.

"What?"

"I can't find my gun. You have my gun, Amigo?"

"What? You have a gun?"

"Of course. You have my gun? No? Maybe I drop it in the back," he said, and opened the back door. He bent down and looked inside. There was nothing there. He stood upright and put his hand in the other pocket of his coat. He smiled broadly. He pulled a small revolver out and waved it by my stomach. "I got it all the time, Amigo," he laughed. "You sure you don't want to dance?"

I shook my head.

He put the gun away, pulled the pint from his back pocket, took a long, healthy swallow, and wiped his mouth with the back of his hand. "I see you later then. You like the shrimp salad." And he walked away.

# Unexpected Companions in the African Rain Forest

*by Tim Schell*

Just after the season's first rain I laced up my brown, dusty tennis shoes and left the town of M'Baiki behind me as I ran up the laterite road into the rain forest of the Central African Republic. It was late afternoon and the road was crowded with men and women returning to town from their fields. Some of them carried bananas, some oranges, others manioc or firewood or full pans of water balanced precariously on their heads. I was in M'Baiki as a Peace Corps volunteer to teach English to African students in the local high school, and I knew the country and its people fairly well.

I ran uphill, forcing a tired smile for those who were watching. It was humid and I was out of shape, but I'd always loved to run in the rain; now that the rainy season had come again, I was excited. Six months of toiling through dry, dusty weather was behind me.

I passed the last mud-brick dwellings of the village and entered the forest, following a narrow path. The myriad forest sounds somehow made the going easier—the cackling of strange birds, the squealing of monkeys and the rhythmic hacking of machetes into wood. And then I heard laughter.

In drawing closer to the sound, I rounded a sharp bend, looked up, blinked, then rubbed my eyes and looked again. I had come upon a pygmy village. Though no one was in sight, I could tell who lived in the settlement by the rounded leaf huts that looked like miniature igloos. The entrances to the huts were so small that I would have had to crawl on all fours to get through one of them. I also knew that pygmies were nomadic hunters who ordinarily live deep in the rain forest, so this had to be a temporary settlement. They would hunt

---

*Tim Schell is now teaching English in Japan.*

enough to sustain themselves here while acquiring pots, pans and tobacco in the village, but they wouldn't stay this close to civilization any longer than was necessary.

I heard more laughter and singing, and finally I saw the pygmies: women pounding manioc in huge mortars; men sharpening spears and repairing hunting nets; children chasing one another in games. They saw me, too, and were silent for just a moment before they began cheering.

Whether you are running in the New York Marathon or in the African bush, cheering helps, and I picked up my pace. Then two men started after me and, though I was going at as fast a pace as I could handle, they caught up with me easily.

With a pygmy on each side I started up a long hill out of the settlement. Neither of them said a word, but the crowd started to cheer louder and also erupted with some of the loudest laughter I've ever heard. When I looked back, I saw that some of the villagers were actually holding their sides while others were rolling on the ground. I looked at my two companions and saw that they were smiling shyly. I supposed they weren't yet sure whether I shared the general mood of hilarity. I did, so I smiled back, and the three of us ran off into the forest.

These were rugged little men. Though a good head and a half shorter than I (I'm 5' 10"), they were powerfully built, and they were runners. It made sense that they should be, because they spend their lives pursuing game and going mile after mile in search of new hunting areas. Their hunting technique calls for a great deal of running in extraordinarily difficult conditions. The pygmies set up huge nets in the forest, and while several of their number hide behind the nets, the rest run for miles through the bush scaring up small game and chasing it to the nets. Those who lie in wait kill the animals with spears or poison arrows shot from crossbows. The run I was straining through with these two was, for them, nothing more than an easy warmup.

They were barefoot, but that didn't matter to them in the least, even though the trail was strewn with jagged rocks. It was an inspiration to see them floating along; soon I forgot my own fatigue. We were running at a much faster pace than I could ever have held alone. Whenever I turned to look at one of my partners, all I saw, besides an effortless stride, was a wide, happy smile, revealing sharply pointed teeth that were darkly stained by tobacco and berries.

They could have run circles around me if they'd cared to, a fact they knew as well as I, but they wanted companionship, not competition. They were so anxious to make this clear that when I spit, they spit. When I cleared my throat, they did, too, and when my breathing became labored—and it became very labored—they pretended that theirs was, too.

We ran that way for several kilometers, through small fields that had been cleared by hand from the dense forest. We passed an orange grove and crossed a narrow bridge over a small creek that would soon be running full again. Soon mango trees appeared, so we were nearly back to town, and I knew that my running companions would have no desire to visit civilization. It was nearly dusk when they turned away toward their settlement. Before they left me, the one on my right extended his left hand, the one on my left his right, and we clasped hands firmly. Then they were gone.

That wasn't the last time I ran with the pygmies, though. Three or four times a week I would pass their village and hear the same cheers and laughter, and my two friends would drop whatever they were doing to join me. Sometimes one or two other men came along. It lasted for about three months, until one day I ran down the path and discovered that the village was gone. They had moved on. I moved on myself a short time later, but whenever I run in the rain, I remember them fondly. I hope that's how they remember me.

# Grass Huts Up Close

*by Bill Finnegan*

The scene is a small but heavily populated island in the Indian Ocean. My lady and I rent a picture-postcard little house for somewhat less per month than we paid for a post office box back home. However, country living at six degrees north latitude turns out to involve more than a technicolor seafloor and the perfect papaya.

Basically, it's...basic. Fancy home improvements like plumbing, electricity, glass windows, and Saran Wrap are unknown, while their simple predecessors are not quite as simple as they look. Cooking in clay pots over a fire of permanently damp coconut husks, sifting endless sacks of rice for invisible tooth-cracking rocks, juggling food supplies to stay ahead of the hourly advance of rot: these are a few of the techniques that should be learned quickly if one doesn't want to starve.

What about just picking fruit from the trees? Well, somebody *owns* the trees. We've got mango, papaya, wild honey, cinnamon, coconut, jackfruit, banana, wood apple, cashew, and countless spices and herbs within a long arm's reach of our back door. But if a single banana were to disappear tonight, a certain farmer would be here at dawn, and not on a social call. It may look like wilderness, but it's agriculture, and of the intensive variety.

Consider the coconut. I have counted no fewer than 53 different uses for the products of the coconut tree over the past two years—everything from alcohol to retaining walls, sandpaper to cooking oil to twine, not to mention the traditional grass shack, which is in reality made entirely from the coconut tree. If and when the global civilization you hail from blows

---

*When this was written Bill Finnegan was an "occasional" writer who had worked as a railroad brakeman before he left for the Indian Ocean. Now he's a free-lance writer in Hollywood.*

up, there will be whole populations hardly inconvenienced, and this one will be one of them.

At the opposite end of the utility spectrum, one finds in this village the slow-witted, soft-handed foreigner. Overconscious of this contrast himself, the pale nouveau pioneer considers learning how to fish in the local style but is put off by the prospect of whole nights in a tiny outrigger miles out to sea. Instead, he apprentices himself to a graceful young fruit picker named Sarath, whose specialty is coconuts. Coconuts grow between 15 and 90 feet off the ground. At the local going wage of something less than a penny per tree, that means a lot of up and down for the workaday harvester. And Sarath goes up a four-story tree with such a swift, smooth succession of scissorlike movements—feet tied together with twine, machete hooked casually through his loincloth—that you hardly notice that he's left the ground before the great green nuts start thumping out of the sky. It's really something to see.

His student, sad to say, is less impressive. So far, I can only get to the tops of rather short and not terribly vertical trees, and must give scratched thighs and arms several days off between lessons. But surely we didn't come halfway around the world to frazzle ourselves mastering arcane skills. What about that old tropical languor, that hammock strung in the trade winds, Jimmy Buffett, and piña coladas?

Well, for purposes of languor, I think I'd stay in front of my electric fan in Fresno. Because you'll get no rest in the hard-core tropics. Mainly it's the bugs. Fleas, flies, ants, gnats, ticks, spiders, cane bugs, the ubiquitous mosquito, and a few million other species whose names in English I do not know. A mosquito net, a hammock, various sprays and salves, maybe a second-hand moon-walk suit, help. But the law of the jungle is, alas, *keep moving.*

Last night, while trying to light a kerosene lamp, I had match heads, lighted and unlighted, flying everywhere (local matches take a more delicate touch than I've got). One flew into the can that contains a leg of our kitchen table. The can is there for the old "moat to keep the ants down" trick. Except it was not full of water because our ants have learned to swim mere water—it was full of kerosene. We are calling the result "Molotov table leg," and we're lucky to still have a house.

The village washerman, a strange, old, toothless, giggling character, comes around on these beautiful winter mornings and quickly works the conversation around from laundry to holidays. These are not exactly Buddhist celebrations approaching, but the washerman seems to know all about them. He giggles and hisses and works himself up into quite an indiscreet frenzy, chanting, "I want Christmas present! I want Christmas present!"

What can a poor haole do? We writhe and say, "Heh-heh, yeah, maybe. Get the sarongs cleaner and we'll think about it." When he's gone, we set our jaws and tell each other, "No way." But the pressure is there, from people and termites and monkeys and microbes. You are never alone.

As for romance, the wilting heat and oceanic humidity lay that fantasy to rest rather quickly. A sarong or lavalava may seem designed to come off at a smoldering glance, but that's only your inept job of tying, nothing more exciting. And your physical condition after spending any length of time at this latitude will complete the discouragement to dalliance.

Sea ulcers, fever, diarrhea, sunburn, constant headaches, and salt deficiency cramps; scabies, pleurisy, multiple rashes, raging infections in every scratch and mosquito bite: these are daily fare. Typhoid fever, dengue fever, malaria, and hepatitis are the major league illnesses the two of us have suffered in the past year alone. And we're still up and around. The tropics bring you back to your body all right—like a world war might help you to notice your national boundaries.

For reasons you don't even pretend to understand, you're 10,000 miles from home—and that doesn't begin to describe the distances involved. At the moment we are sweating buckets inside a mosquito net, listening to a neighbor woman howl at the moon. It's midnight, and the house reeks of mildew and coconut oil. It's starting to rain for the 43rd consecutive night, and I can hear mice and fruit bats scrabbling for dry spots in the thatch above my head. Under the floor the sound of digging signals the return of the hated iguana, determined to build its nest there. I laugh at the thought that I will have to call the iguana hunter in the morning, yet the jungled night out there is no joke. For beyond the maddening whine of the mosquitoes, the endless rustling and muttering and occasional screams, teem the sources of real strangeness, of fierce superstition and ritual magic. And at some point anthropology goes out the window.

These days, when our best educated neighbor, a kid bound for the capitol and college next year, points down our well and describes the spirit who lives there, we listen. And when he says that his grandfather's family was once decimated by this same spirit for an offense against its former residence, a bo tree behind our house, I know that I will tread lightly around that tree thenceforth.

Finally, then, it's me, the old San Fernando Valley suburbanite, seriously considering sponsoring an exorcism for the woman who is bewitched (and I'm hoping for a discount by providing the iguana blood myself). It's me spinning myths for incredulous villagers about microwave ovens and sit-down toilets and a telephone in every home (while dreaming nightly about deli sandwiches and about sleeping under blankets again). It's me looking at the outside world through the wrongwise telescope of a two-month-old *Time* magazine, while baffled by envious letters from old friends about my exotic new life. Finally, I am the one who requires exorcism, relief from the afflictions of too much dream life. Or so it seems as the monsoon drums, the iguana digs, and the mad lady howls at the moon.

# Odyssey of a Heretic

*by Joe Kennedy Adams*

In 1958 I received a U.S. Public Health Service Fellowship for research in "the use of psychotomimetic drugs in the study of psychological processes." The drug I was chiefly interested in was LSD, which at that time was so little known to the general public that if you said "LSD" to a police officer he would either look completely puzzled or else assume that you were referring to a type of boat used during World War II. My first subject was myself and I had an interesting trip, though not as spectacular or ecstatic as some which came later. Don Jackson, a psychiatrist famous for his work with families containing "schizophrenic" members, was at that time involved in setting up the Mental Research Institute (as a new and relatively independent part of the Palo Alto Medical Research Foundation), and at my suggestion we applied for and received a $30,000 two-year grant from the National Institute of Mental Health to study the uses of LSD and similar drugs in personality evaluation. Although for administrative reasons Don was designated as Principal Investigator, I was the actual director of the drug project and had virtually a free hand, especially as my salary came from the Fellowship and was completely independent of the Mental Research Institute.

Our subjects included "normal" volunteers, among whom were many psychologists and psychiatrists and others such as Allan Ginsberg, who first took LSD under my direction. (Allen was one of the most conscientious and generous subjects in writing up his experiences and their aftermath—most of the mental-health professionals gave us exactly nothing.) We also conducted sessions for people who were in psychotherapy, always at their request and with the consent and cooperation

---

*Joe Kennedy Adams is a retired psychologist who lives in the San Francisco bay area.*

of their therapists.

I took LSD myself many times and in late December, 1959, I had the same surprise that many other people have had—a trip that was totally unexpected and in some ways catastrophic. I was plunged into a depression that persisted after the direct effects of the drug had worn off; I realized that I hadn't even known what "depression" meant up to then. I thought suicide was superfluous because I would die within a few days anyway and that furthermore I should.

This depression began to lift during the fifth day, and then was abruptly and dramatically terminated by a righteous rage that was so intense I felt as though I were on fire, yet with a pleasure all over my body that I can compare only with an orgasm. This experience was accompanied by technicolor visions and feelings of omnipotence and demonic cleverness. The account given by Jung of the experience of the magician archetype flashed through my mind—it seemed bizarre, however, that I could have a "realistic" thought of this kind when I was so absorbed in the experience itself. The rage lasted only a few seconds, while I was walking back to my car, after buying a jacket to wear in the snow, but I continued to feel extremely strange and to have vivid fantasies. Nevertheless, I found that I could control my behavior very well, and I drove home with no difficulty.

My two-and-a-half year old son greeted me at the door and seemed delighted with the change he sensed—he put up his little fists and said, "Box with me, Daddy." While playing with my son I experienced a conflict as to whether I wanted to be a magician or a human being, and when I decided in favor of the latter the magician vanished as suddenly as he had appeared (just as Jung says!).

During the next 60 hours, however, the magician came and went a number of times, and I had many other strange and weird experiences over which I seemed to have no control whatsoever, although I continued to be able to control my behavior (drive a car, talk to people, etc.). I knew very well that I was having what many people call a psychotic experience and I wondered whether I would ever emerge from it—a frightening thought, to put it mildly.

When I woke up one morning and the autonomous experience was gone I felt completely on top of the world. I felt renewed, reborn—mentally and physically. In fact, I felt so good and full of energy and uninhibited that my behavior changed markedly and abruptly, and the people who knew me became alarmed. I charged around having the time of my life, taking control of every situation and turning it into more or less of a circus. Acting on impulse was so satisfying that I didn't want to stop, not realizing how dangerous behavior of this kind can be.

For many reasons impulsive behavior makes enemies, the most dangerous of whom are people who will not tell you they don't like the way you are acting and/or they consider it very inappropriate. Such persons often do you great harm, sometimes with the conscious intent of being helpful. My judgments of how other people were perceiving me and how they received my communications were extremely poor, not only because of a lack of direct and honest feedback, but also because I had so little interest in hearing or thinking about anything other people were saying.

After hastily scribbling a set of earth-shaking discoveries modestly titled "Psychology," I called up a Very Important Person whom I had never met, obtained an immediate appointment, hurried to his office, and slammed my masterpiece on his desk. When he looked it over and indicated that he did not want to be involved, I told him that if he wasn't interested I would go to the White House or to Sandoz (the Swiss corporation which manufactured LSD—he probably thought I meant a circus strong man).

Immediately after I left his office this VIP contacted Don Jackson and insisted that I receive some "help." Don persuaded me to see a psychiatrist ("someone who can evaluate this situation objectively" was the way he tactfully put it), whom I then saw almost every day for two months. At that point I stopped going because I regarded the whole thing as a waste of money. Even the tranquilizers and sedatives that were prescribed did not bring me down—I was on a continual high and loved every minute of the exciting adventure that life had become.

Although I continued to conduct LSD sessions, I lost most

of my interest in drugs and instead became focused on emotions and social processes, especially those which attempt to force individuals into roles that others consider appropriate. Although everyone who knew me well was appalled at the change in my behavior (except my son), I met some new people who found me lively and amusing; these people tended to be aggressive and unafraid of others. I wrote long, raving letters and several articles, each of which I considered a priceless gem. This behavior went on for many months before I more or less came down to earth and began to be high only part of the time instead of all the time.

About one year after my righteous rage I had another psychotic experience, but this time in a different and even stranger way. I had been keyed up for two or three days and had been furiously trying to put some ideas and facts together which seemed to have some important though unclear connections with each other. One Sunday afternoon, as I was pacing back and forth thinking, these ideas and facts began to fall into place in a way that increased my excitement to such a crescendo that my brain went into a veritable jam session, and I experienced hallucinations and uncanny emotions.

This time, however, my behavior as well as my experience got out of control in the sense that I lost all judgment about how others would perceive me. Many things happened, but to make a long story short, soon after the experience began I took my clothes off and started to run down the street naked, thinking I had solved the "Riddle of the Universe" and that everybody who saw me would realize that the Millennium had arrived. My Mission was interrupted when I was intercepted in the driveway by a psychiatrist, who somehow got me back into the house and then left me alone.

Shortly thereafter I heard a siren and three uniformed policemen came in, tied me down on a stretcher, carried me into a long ambulance with a light on top, and hurried me to Twin Pines (now known as Belmont Hills), a private sanitarium in Belmont, California. I still remember with gratitude what the young policeman who sat by me during the ride said to me: "You know what? I like you!" (One of the others had shoved me into a chair and said, "Stay there and shut up or we'll cut your head off." I didn't follow his orders but fortunately he didn't carry out his threat.)

At Twin Pines I was injected with tranquilizers but continued to cut up so much that I was strapped to the bed for several days. I growled and snarled like an animal, gnawed the leather restraining straps halfway through, pissed in the bed, encountered three gods, and at various times thought I was in hell, that the head nurse was a witch, that I was on worldwide tv and had to show everybody what an ass I had been, that I was in the hands of Communists (I am a native Texan), and that I was the subject of an experiment being carried on jointly by the U.S.A. and Russia (with one shift of aides being the Russian team and the other the U.S. team).

I also managed to run out the door onto the grounds, again stark naked, yelling, "This is not a hospital!" and not long afterwards told the other inmates, "Soon we'll all be able to get out of this place." In such ways I established a reputation as one of the craziest patients Twin Pines had ever had. As my psychiatrist told my wife, "We don't ordinarily have patients quite that disturbed."

Within two weeks I became reasonably clear about who and where I was and had no trouble. My privileges increased and I was allowed to leave only one month after entering. For several years following that I was "fanatical" about the treatment of inmates in so-called mental hospitals. Why? Because even with the many advantages I had, this was still by far the roughest experience of my life and the hardest to recover from. Although I had worked in mental hospitals, for the first time the enormous obstacles to recovery faced by the average inmate hit me in the face, so to speak.

I have used the term "many advantages" but in a sense only one really counted because without it the others would have been either nonexistent or of little importance. This advantage was that my wife refused to consent to electric shock treatments, despite considerable pressure on her to do so. She was warned, "If this psychotic process is allowed to continue he will never be the same again." At Twin Pines a large majority of the inmates, very few of whom were psychotic in the sense which I was, received electric shock, and it was also given on an outpatient basis.

I am very happy to report that the warning I would never

again be the same was a true prediction. Psychotic episodes are disintegrations which provide an opportunity for reintegration at new levels. (These levels are not necessarily higher—some may be higher and some lower, quite aside from differing judgments which arise from differing values in living and different concepts of human nature. I do not claim to be on any "high" level overall and have no interest in striving toward any such exalted state.) Jung stated this principle long ago, claiming that psychotic episodes are the quickest though the most hazardous paths to what he called "individuation." Despite the fact that this principle has been recognized for centuries in the Far East and despite the recent work of Ronald Laing and others, the idea that there are constructive aspects of psychosis is still unaccepted in practice by the vast majority of "mental health" experts. Thus, not only are large numbers of individuals prevented from developing in accordance with inner-directed growth, but also an enormous amount of creative energy that could be extremely valuable to our society is lost. From asylums in the true sense—that is, places of refuge from the world which could be entered and left voluntarily—much helpful knowledge, wisdom, and beneficial efforts could emerge.

# Locked-Up Feelings Behind Bars

*by Louis Lab*

I'm getting out of prison soon. Before Christmas. I wonder what it will be like, the affection and all. Not too long ago, through "understandable" error, I was thrown into special-segregation—the hole—in probably the most vicious and tension-haunted penitentiary in the United States. It is the U.S. Penitentiary at Lompoc, California.

It is the one that has doubled its perimeter fences and added extra rolls of concertina razor-wire. And it has raised its security level and beefed up its tower armament. All of that has happened since Christopher Boyce chased his private falcon—and then disappointed a lot of sometimes confused legend-makers. It is a brutal world in the U.S.P. I spent the better part of a month there with the hardest of the hard. Some live there for a lifetime, however long that may be. But more about that in a minute.

I have been around the federal prison system. I lived in a maximum security Correctional Center for many months while Patty Hearst was there five floors below me. At the La Tuna Penitentiary, Texas, I spent some time in that mostly Hispanic prison. While I was there, a special unit entertained an ABSCAM figure—the unit had originally been built for a man named Joe Valachi. Later it had hosted Jimmy "The Weasel" Fratianno. Transferred to Terminal Island, California, I worked daily with Dr. Jeffrey McDonald, a former Green-Beret physician, and Stanley Rifkin, a would-be computer wizard and diamond merchant. I had discovered this world to be a tough, scareful life where each action is measured by bits of parceled-out favors and dominated by thoughts of advantage.

---

*Shortly after this was written, Louis Lab was released from the U.S. Penitentiary at Lompoc, California, after serving a sentence for the receipt of illegal gratuities, and was assigned to a halfway house.*

Men die in prison and violently. Four reasons dominate—things lent and not returned; drugs used, abused, and payment neglected; the razor edge of racism; and the secret not-so-secret homosexual liaison.

Everyone is involved. Kindness becomes the mark of weakness and an invitation to extortion. To refuse drugs quickly selects your social order outside the security of power-groups. To remain racially liberal is an unacceptable and dangerous non-choice. An accidental lingering eye-contact rips at the fabric of psychosexual stability. Sides must be chosen.

Men have died violently around me. The groans of one man entwined horribly with the snarl of another in the dormitory darkness. Long moments later, the flaring lights found an elderly man three beds from me, garroted with a guitar string, a dime in his palm and spattered with black ink.

Another time a man sat a few seats from me in the theater. There was a quiet scuffle, men moving away a measured distance and a thump. When the lights rose he was slumped forward. His head seemed supported on the chair-back in front of him. A sharpened spike had been driven into the lower back of his head and protruded from the top of his skull—that was the support.

There were no witnesses to these and so many other acts. Prison is not amenable to witnesses. Affection and concern must be placed on a very high shelf during these times. The first priority cannot be forgotten—*one must survive* to get out of prison and be with his family again.

I read a study once and it chilled me. It said that after perhaps one year of prison, a man's appetite for affection begins to fade, to brown out. It is like avocados, Beluga caviar, and Dom Perignon '55—the taste dulls with time and your subconscious mind kicks an ever-thickening layer of dirt over it. They're buried. How permanent is that interment? Is it like a hairspring that, once bent, never again regains its original tensile liveliness? Will feeling green again in spring, I wondered?

Touching is not done in prison. A few men do. But they touch in *their* ways and a man who is not gay vigorously avoids the slightest taint. I felt it in myself. I had thought that affection was mostly dead (except for the too-fleeting aurora of a family visit). I had assumed that the prison's affection vacuum was as devoid of the warmth of emotional energy as the intergalactic abyss. But this other place—the "hole"—chilled through bone.

The cellblock to which I was taken was two tiers high. There were no outside windows in the cells in special-segregation. Across—about 30 feet from my cell bars and behind welded-wire mesh—were high grated windows that permitted hazy daylight. A "recreation" privilege was granted, two men at a time, for 30 minutes each day. That was the time allotted to shower and walk the "freeway" (the narrow runway that faces the long row of cells.) Sometimes recreation was forgotten. No guard was allowed to walk the freeway during recreation. The danger was too great. When all were locked in their cells, the meals arrived on trays. All human functions—sleeping, eating, eliminating, body hygiene—were resolved in the six-by-eight concrete-walled cell.

There were two parts to I-Block and this part was reserved for the most violent and serious offenders. The man to my right (who was at first only a disembodied voice) was a "hold-over," placed in segregation while waiting for transportation to the penitentiary in Marion, Illinois. He will most likely spend a few years there in "close" custody. He recently killed a man. He was called Kabo (he said it meant Cash Box) and he had been in prison for 24 of his 41 years. He was my recreation "partner."

On my left lived Bo and he was 27 years old. Bo had been in prison for eight years and was to be released in only five months. He put himself in the hole.

When a man gets "short" in the penitentiary—a short-timer—the others around him develop intense jealousies. Whatever his evasions, the short-timer is soon chosen for some "action" (the killing or maiming of another man for retribution or retaliation). Choosing not to take part in an action is a choice against a powerful group. That is dangerous indeed. Thus a man who is short may suddenly find himself with the quick discomfort of many more prison years, the result of a new, enlarged sentence because of his action. Careers are made.

But a few judicious men wish to leave prison in the worst way. They may put themselves quietly into self-imposed special-segregation during those last six months to a year. Bo was one of those who had made that hard choice and, for a few weeks, was a friend to me.

Below me (my cell was on the second lever) lived Rifaat. Kabo, Bo, and Rifaat were black men who clearly understood the power factions. The U.S.P. at Lompoc has them all. There are the D.C. Blacks, the Aryan Brotherhood, the L.A. Blacks, the Mexican Mafia, the Texas Syndicate, the California Blacks, the Italian Mafia... Kabo, Bo, and Rifaat spoke another language with one another that was not English. It was designed for private communications in prison, a sort of super pig-Latin. Kabo was slow at the language, Bo sharp, and Rifaat a quiet man of few words.

I spoke to Kabo one evening a few days after my arrival. It was shortly after the Falklands' debacle and I had noticed that current events take an often-fascinating twist in prison. Kabo had been speaking at length in a tirade of grunts and roars about himself as a mercenary soldier, were he "on the streets." With Kabo, oaths and profanity were ultimate and every second or third word. He was a surly, dangerous man and I made an error.

"If I was out on them streets, I'd get me $35 million in gold ripped together 'n buy me a whole pot-load o' explosives, plastics 'n M-16s, grenades, rockets, bazooks, 'n blow the whole top of the island away! Then I'd move in with some action and have me a whole island to m'sef!" he roared.

Thirty-five or more shouting voices offered comments. Kabo roared loudest and best.

"Ah, Kabo," I offered hesitantly (since I lived next to him, I could speak quietly and with reserve). But everyone somehow heard this stranger. There was silence. "Ah, if you had $35 million in gold, Kabo, why not just buy yourself an island? Then you don't have to blow up anyone..."

"You ain' heard a word! You ain' listen'n, man! It's all about action...power...blowing 'em all away!" There was a jungle silence for several seconds and my heart froze. "How much time you carry, man?"

My mind had glued itself to truth. "Ah, well, ah, another year. Then I'm going..."

"Aaagh...a year!" he snarled. His voice softened to the staccato of an automatic weapon. "I'm goin' jolt you, man. I'm goin' pull you under the dirt, man. You better slide, man, 'cause at rec I'm rippin' and tearin' out your air and coughin' away, man!"

Kabo already carried three consecutive life sentences and would never again see freedom. He did not like to take advice from a person who was "short." I spoke later with the guard. I no longer recreated with Kabo. In fact, I suddenly felt a need to recreate alone. I owed it to myself, my wife and children. Only a month before, a man had been slashed up in this very cellblock by his recreation partner.

A note slipped through the bars of my cell by a hand to my left. It was Bo. I played chess with Bo, calling out the moves, and I had bought him some cigarets and a few stamps because he had no commissary money.

*Don't say nothing. Nothing. These people don't play fair in here no way. It's trouble. Just keep quiet. Nothing.*

Solid advice.

A man arrived shortly after I did. He lived below me and was called Hippie. Hippie read a lot. I had known Hippie at prison camp before I went to the hole—we both played tennis and I was happy to hear a familiar voice. Hippie gets in trouble at work sometimes and visits the hole.

One evening a collective discussion focused on exacting a revenge on a man who had stolen a radio from another man's cell out in the penitentiary population. Two would hold the victim from behind. One would cover his mouth. The radio-bereft man would cut. And cut. The detail was endless. It hurt my ears, this animal house, and it must have hurt Hippie's as well.

Hippie was a tall, thin man, a vegetarian with Ben Franklin spectacles. He walked in a swinging shuffle, and I can see him in my mind's eye as he would shamble to the bars of his cell.

"You men must be really proud of yourselves," I heard him say with the beginnings of horror, "discussing the taking of another man's life that way."

His gentle words shattered the talk. A long moment of silence passed. Then came an hour of animated discussion: the killing of Hippie. Hippie said nothing more.

*What a fool you were, Hippie,* I raged to myself over and over. I paced and heard them and clutched at the bars, agitated beyond despair.

I had always held good feelings for Hippie. (Could this recklessly courageous and profound remark be part of a higher design, I wondered helplessly at one moment?) Hippie was miraculously released from the hole the next morning *before* recreation.

But I stayed longer. And I was silent. I read and played quiet chess with Bo. Later the Bureau of Prisons discovered their "procedural" error. I was not supposed to be in a maximum security special-segregation unit. I was supposed to be in a minimum security camp unrestrained by any *physical* barriers— only those self-imposed restraints of returning unencumbered again to society.

When I saw Hippie again in more private circumstances (in the same camp where I now reside) I told him a thing or two. Actually two. He was a fool, I said, and that moment I had admired him for it.

I'm going home...just before Christmas. I wonder what it's going to be like, the affection and all.

# Love Behind Glass, One Dollar

*by Marianne Adams*

My name is Marianne, and I work in a three-level sex emporium on Times Square. This is my job: I sit on a stool in a glass booth, like a phone booth, and talk with men on the phone.

The men stand in an adjoining booth, separated from me by two sheets of glass and a vinyl curtain. When a man puts a Susan B. Anthony dollar in the slot on his side of the glass, the curtain goes up and he can see me open my kimono. The curtain stays up for 55 seconds, and it is up to me to keep him there dropping dollars. The company and I split each dollar 60-40 (in the company's favor).

Most of our customers are men. They come to look, to fondle themselves, and to fantasize. There is something for everyone— old widowers with no one to turn to, horny businessmen on their lunch hour, young kids cutting school who just want to see what a female looks like up close. There are foot freaks, nose lovers, even some who want to hear detailed descriptions of other men's organs.

We act out their fantasies with them, becoming for a moment their mothers, sisters, first girlfriends, mistresses, or slaves.

We get tourists from Japan, Germany, Saudi Arabia, even exotic Los Angeles. All are welcome. Sometimes women come to look at us, and they are welcome too.

But there are two unwelcome groups. One is the WAP organization—Women Against Pornography. Their appearance belies their name—it is impossible to look at them and not think Ladies Against Pornography, as in "Ladies' Auxiliary" or "Ladies' Sewing Circle." One sees white gloves where no gloves are as they lead guided tours through the building, pointing out the attractions with enthusiastic disgust.

---

*This story is from the "Other Voices" column—a reader-written one—from the* Village *Voice. Marianne Adams is a pseudonym. Neither the* Voice *nor this editor knows where she is today.*

WAP gets a lot of media coverage and professes to be concerned about exploitation of women. Yet these ladies come up here and stare at us as they might stare at copulating dogs. I smile at them and wave, and they look away quickly and huddle together instead of smiling back.

I once saw one of them standing outside the men's room, obviously needing to relieve herself but reluctant to go in. I came out of my booth and offered to take her to the ladies' room inside our dressing room. She looked at me in utter horror and scurried back to the herd; apparently she would rather wet her pants than deal with her "exploited sisters."

WAP's mission is to close down places like the one where I work, stop the showing of X-rated movies, close down massage parlors, and stop publication of certain magazines. There are overtones of fascism in that. At best, it is a criminally naive position. WAP doesn't realize (or doesn't care) that exploitation of women in the sex business increases proportionately as the participants are driven underground.

I am only a dilettante—picking up experience and easy money, pushing my artistic career the rest of the time. I go home every night to the same man and cook dinner in domestic peace and tranquility. So I am not too susceptible to the whirlpool that pulls women in this life deeper and deeper into the sewer. My first week here I was approached by three pimps—they come into the booths—and I politely (very politely) declined invitations to drink, do some cocaine, have a little talk. After a while they left me alone. But not everyone here has the same options dropped on me by birthright as a white middle-class American female.

In our establishment, one of two in this building, there are more than 20 women employed at any given time. The managers are all women, too, who have worked their way up from the booths. That's 20 women who can say no to a pimp because they don't have to worry about feeding their children. Another 20 are employed downstairs in a show just like ours, and hundreds more work along the strip. There are five porters on every floor, paid well above minimum wage. There are silver dollar men who receive a salary and a percentage of what they sell. There are barkers, security guards, mechanics and electricians, all working on the books and paying taxes, all employed in a city full of unemployed. We are a serious link in the economic chain, and to demand that we close down with no thought to the consequences is unrealistic.

And what about the customers? If we abolish prostitutes and peep shows and X-rated magazines, instead of trying to change the repressive climate that created a need for all this in the first place, then these people will be out on the street looking for their satisfaction, and surely it is wild enough out there already.

The other unwelcome group of visitors come to us from the city of New York—the Vice Squad. Once a week or so, undercover police tour the peep shows until they have filled a truck with dangerous females. Those arrested are read no rights or charges. They spend anywhere from 2 to 24 hours in jail, depending on the day's depth of paperwork, and then the company comes and bails them out.

The girls circulate myths to try to convince themselves there is some way to avoid a bust—they can't take you if you don't touch yourself, they can't open their pants, they have to tell you if they're cops, and so on. The truth is that "they" can do whatever "they" want, and when pressed for time "they" have taken fully clothed women out of the building.

Recently a woman was raped by a man claiming to be a cop. He flashed a badge to get her out of the building and then dragged her to a motel at gunpoint. Typically, she had been too afraid of antagonizing a policeman to ask to inspect his identification.

More unconscionable than the terrorization of the working girl is the waste of desperately needed taxpayers' money. Murderers, pimps, pushers, and dangerous people of every description walk the streets of New York as if they owned the city. Where is the rationale for expending time and manpower on us, clogging the courts with women who sit behind glass, open their negligees for 55 seconds, then close them again?

When a man comes to see us in the booths, we flatter him, cajole him, brighten his day, and make him feel better than he did when he came in—all for just a few dollars. Now, is that really so terrible?

# Please Sign Off. You're Fired!
*by Dr. Frish*

We were a fairly typical middle-class family. I was working in a high-paying high-technology job, and my wife was taking care of the house and kids. Then I got "impacted by RIF."

RIF is the latest technology developed in Silicon Valley. It is sometimes difficult to keep up with all the innovation, but to know about RIF is a must. We all may be affected; maybe we are already affected but do not yet know. It happened like this:

I was sitting in my office three months ago, in that high-tech high-pay job, and I was worried. I was writing a program for a computer model of our latest product. This program, when finished, would make the computer simulate the motion of the product parts. Such models allow one to "try out" different designs by changing the model parameters. When the actual prototype is built and something goes wrong, the company can use the model to "de-bug" the hardware. We look for the differences between the prototype and the model and gradually change the real machine to emulate its image, represented in the computer by my program.

I had written such models before, but this time my progress was slow. One reason was that I was worried. I had reason to worry. Two weeks before, all employees had received a memo from the president. That's unusual for a company with 3000 people. Three thousand sheets saying: "We are doing all right. Business is a little slow, but the economy is supposed to pick up any day. So to really make it great, we will have a Reduction In Force."

That's a RIF. The origins of modern RIF technology can be traced back a few years to the concept of the "outplacement department," or Golden Parachute—the graceful elimination

---

*Dr. Frish is a pseudonym for a Silicon Valley (San Francisco bay area) job-seeker. All names in this story have been changed.*

of high-level executives. Today, the mass-produced, cost-effective version, the RIF, is a booming business in Silicon Valley. It is taught in management seminars and overseen by high-powered consultants.

I was sitting in my office trying to work faster, worrying about a new sheet posted on the bulletin board: "Today the workforce will be reduced by 350 people, selected from all departments and levels."

"Oh my," I thought, "that is a 10 percent RIF, quite a cut." At 10 a.m., Kyle, my manager, walked in. He had just returned from a week's vacation and he was full of energy.

"How are you doing with the model?" he asked. "Can I get details?" That was unusual. In most casual conversations he just wanted results. Only when the project had been completed did he ask for the documentation, procedures, all that. This time he even asked me how to enter this particular computer, what manual I used, the password. So I gave him all that, and he left.

I kept on sitting in my office, and this time I was just worrying. This time, I did not try to do anything faster, so I worried better. Kyle came back after lunch.

"Bad news," he said, and read me a letter: "Unfortunately, you, too, have been impacted by RIF..."

He had a checklist of things to do:

"Give me your badge." Check.

"All 'company private data' in this box." Check. Oof.

"Let's go through the bookcase. Your books in this box. The company books stay there." Another check. Another oof.

"They say here I should close the access. How do you do that?" I typed in the proper command for him. The password was usually changed monthly. I retired the old password, turned my back to the terminal and, facing the wall, instructed him to type in the new password of his choice.

As he typed in the new password, my universe shrank. A minute ago I could have called up hundreds of programs, dozens of computers in the Corporate Computer Center, the news in the digital grapevine that crisscrosses the globe. For program exchanges, access to data bases of patents, competitive technology evaluations, reports...the Corporate Computer is used by all. Not by me anymore.

Lately, it was true, I somehow did not fit in. I tried: We have kids. A mortgage to pay, credit cards. All these thoughts were exploding like tiny fireworks inside my head. I was in a state of shock. I saw my manager and office, I mean my ex-manager and ex-office, as if from a distance. I did not have any time to pause and feel the whirl of emotions.

"I really want you to meet these consultants. It's important that you meet them today," Kyle was saying.

Perhaps they had some message for me, I thought. I hoped that it would be like waking up from a nightmare to find out that it was not real, just a dream. I wanted to hurry so as not to miss the message, but I had forms in front of me.

"Here, sign this," Kyle directed.

"I always read things before signing them," I said, and tried to concentrate on the piece of paper before me: "... will not disclose to..."

"You already signed that," Kyle interrupted. "It is the employment contract. We just need it on file." So here I was, making a fuss about something I had already signed. Those consultants I had to meet immediately were waiting. So I signed and started going through my desk.

"This calculator was bought for me by the company," I said, pulling out a TI 59. "When I was transferred from Colorado I was allowed to take it with me."

"That goes here, on the company pile." Kyle did not feel too comfortable, either. As I was putting the next item, a battery-operated pencil sharpener, on the company pile, he said, "You may keep that." I guess he wanted to make the situation in which we both were caught more human. The resulting effect was the opposite, but I did not argue.

Finally the two boxes were filled with "personal effects," mostly books. With visible hesitation, Kyle helped me carry them through a hall past the shocked stares of my colleagues, and to the car. Finally I was led to "meet the consultants."

Their message was rather simple:

(1) Don't jump on the phone to call all your friends; you will need them later, after you think about all this.

(2) Do tell your family.

(3) Tomorrow, report to Building L. We will have a workshop for all of you.

As this conversation was going on, other managers were bringing in other RIFees; I took the unnecessary map showing the location of Building L, and went home. I could not picture myself explaining to my children, 7 and 14 years old, what had happened. So I jumped on the phone and called my friends.

The next day, in Building L, some 70 ex-employees filled the "management training room." The consultants were expert. Each place had a name plate, a blue binder, and a pencil. The first statement they made was: "Each time you change jobs, you should expect a 10 percent increase in salary." That news created a carnival atmosphere.

The idea of bringing all the victims into the same room was a good one. People expressed their emotions, mostly anger. "I was 15 years with this company," said one. That meant that he had worked here from the beginning, when the company was one of the early miracles of high tech.

All kinds of people were present in the room: young and old, men and women, whites and blacks. I recall wondering whether they had the right percentage of Spanish surnames, Orientals, and Native Americans. I was sure that they had balanced the group so that minorities were represented in proper proportions, making discrimination complaints unlikely. Affirmative action in RIFing. Progress.

We filled out a questionnaire. Scored according to rules explained in the blue binder, it classified us into groups. I came out an "intuiter": a chap who worries about the future and tends to smoke a pipe. I was impressed. I used to smoke a pipe, and I was worried, for sure, about the future.

During the lunch break I called the technical library, which is located in my old building. "I have two books from the library," I said. "May I keep them two more weeks, or do I have to return them right away?"

"They must be returned now," said the librarian, her voice quivering with sympathy. I realized that one reason for isolating the RIFees from other employees was to save us a lot of embarrassment and awkwardness. Next morning I walked to the lobby with two books from the library. The guard, a nice fat girl, said, "May I see your badge?" She was supposed to inspect everybody's badges, but she usually did not check mine; she knew me.

63

"No, you can't," I answered, and came over to her desk to explain. It was not necessary. She already knew. "You were laid off?" she said. Again, she felt sorry for me and a little bit guilty. But she had no choice. "I cannot let you in," she said.

"I just need to return these books to the library," I explained. "Perhaps I can just leave them here with you, and you can give them to the librarian."

With this settled, I drove to Building L. Today we would focus on interviewing techniques. One of the RIFees read us a poem he said he written about us.

### *The Ship in a Valley*

*The rats of the Silicon Valley*
*Never leave the sinking ship first.*
*Usually the first to leave is the first mate,*
    *second mate, captain, all other sailors . . .*
*The rats stay and they play a game:*

*The game is called The Rat Race.*
*Rats pretend they handle the ship:*
    *biggest rat climbs the captain's bridge,*
    *smaller rats act as sailors,*
    *the ship keeps on sinking . . .*

*Then the rats keep a council*
    *to decide the Basic Philosophical Question:*
*"Who is to blame?"—and they throw the*
    *guilty rat overboard*
    *and so on—until all the rats leave the ship.*
*The ship sinks, the game ends,*
    *and life goes on; and so on and on . . .*

After that, we heard about self-marketing and interview techniques. We learned of the huge market of "hidden jobs," those positions that "have not yet crystallized into 'official' openings. They exist in shadowy form, business needs that have not yet been fulfilled..."

I pictured these masses of openings, yearning to be filled, and I wondered why I had spent my last eight years here, with this company.

It was the right frame of mind for the next attraction: The Video Tape Interview Training. I knew that I should never discuss my future with the interviewer, unless he was an intuiter, too. I was eager to try the tricks. It was interesting, similar to hearing your recorded voice for the first time. Progress again.

It also helped to project our thoughts onto the future, rather than wasting them on analyzing the past. But that was all the workshop did. We all knew how to write a resume; we all knew that nowadays you get a job through your professional contacts and friends... or you don't.

I have not had many interviews so far, so my polished interviewing technique has not yet borne fruit. But I keep a very positive attitude. I go to all the "open houses" and answer ads with perfect resumes.

The other day, driving by my old building, I remembered that I wanted to withdraw some money from my credit union account. The proper forms used to be in a rack just off the lobby. I stopped by. The old guard, the nice fat girl, was still there.

I explained what I wanted and her eyes remained cold. There was a trace of indignation in her voice. I was no longer a fellow employee who was having some trouble. I was probably one of those desperados who sneak past the personnel department to buttonhole the managers. This time, I was the only one who was embarrassed. Fortunately, one employee who happened to be passing by knew the phone number of the credit union by heart, so I took the number and withdrew with dignity.

I recall some things I did wrong in the past. For example, the problem we had with our custom chip. Suddenly our customers started calling. Some machines, they said, were DOA, "dead on arrival"; some failed shortly afterward. All shipments were put on hold; the vice president for manufacturing put together a task force. It was such an event that a memo was circulated through all engineering groups. "We will evaluate all inputs," the vice president's memo said. It explained the seriousness of the problem and ended with an urgent admonition: "Status me as soon as possible with respect to that!"

I wrote in the margin: "Let's status him now, always with respect." The engineer at the next desk found that funny; I suppose the vice president didn't.

So I practice. After scanning the ads in the paper, I read all the stories on labor and job efficiency. Like this one: "The circle includes employees who get together on a regular basis and share ways in which production can be made more efficient and their jobs enriched..."

I sit down in front of the mirror and say: "Simply the process of having these discussions enhances our job enrichment." I don't stop until I can say it three times in a row with a perfectly straight face.

One of these days, I know, the economy will pick up. I go on looking for a job, and I do some worrying about the future. For the next few months I can still pay the mortgage. I consider picking up the pipe and starting to smoke again.

# The First Cadaver is the Worst Cadaver

*by Lawrence Vincent*

"Okay, gang—raise them up. You're already behind." The teaching faculty didn't bother with any sort of psychological preparation—no lecture or free advice from a sympathetic father figure. The approach was the classic no-nonsense, "Be a trooper" variety. What guidelines there were had been cursorily recited in a monotone: No unauthorized visitors in lab, no picture taking, no eating or smoking, no removal of soft parts. And last but not least, respect the dead. It was the first day of medical school and we were grouped five students to a "tank," physically equipped with spotless blue lab coats, shiny surgical instruments, and the latest edition of the dissecting manual. Hadn't anyone remembered to bring the disposable gloves?

No aspect of medical education is more notorious in the layman's mind than the first year dissection of the human body. That it takes a special breed of individual to stomach it is an absolute myth. For the doctor-to-be, there isn't any choice. The indoctrination begins like a cinder block landing on your head.

Those moments before the first look, just not wanting to look at that damn thing, but realizing it was something I had to do, a hurdle to overcome. Face it, people suffer and die. Besides, I wasn't about to be the jerk who ran out of the room.

We lifted the lid, feigning casualness and ignoring the noticeable silence in the room. The form was draped in a brown tarp and resting in several inches of embalming fluid. When we raised the body to a working position, using a lever on each

---

*This story is from* Harper's Weekly, *published from late 1974 to early 1976, which featured reader-written articles. At that time Lawrence Vincent lived in Shawnee Mission, Kansas. Neither* Harper's Magazine *nor this editor knows where he is today.*

end of the tank, liquid dripped to the tank bottom.

All I was worried about was whether I would faint or throw up. We were acting so cool, but inside everyone was afraid of fainting or throwing up. No one did.

The most courageous group member unshrouded the bottom half, and we stared with a strange objectivity at the two limbs, the feet and toes, the genitals. Cautiously, we touched (why the hell didn't anyone remember to bring gloves?), poked, observed the yellow-brown pallor of the skin, the hair, the monster-like wrinkles and unfoldings of the surface. *This* was a person? The bizarre nonhumanness made it easier: the figure was more akin to a plastic Aurora model or a motion picture prop, except for its cold and leathery surface. It gave like a dry sponge, yet it was wet.

The initial shock wave dissipated. Minutes later we were digging, scraping, slicing, probing. The fat throughout oozed like melted butter; our new coats were becoming filthy with grease and grime. No use in pondering: this was once a human being, who lived and loved, who left people. Had she been baking cookies for her grandchildren a few months earlier? Either consciously or unconsciously we tried not to think about it, concentrating and working on a relatively limited, isolated area.

Sometimes the realization of humanity couldn't be suppressed. Looking at the face for the first time was a major obstacle, one which we avoided confronting for three days. Turning the body over, feeling the entire weight of it, was at first unpleasant, almost dreaded.

"Turn her over? Maybe we should start tomorrow."

"We have an hour left."

"Which way should we lift?"

"Keep the face covered."

The hurdles became smaller and were handled one at a time, with less and less trauma. We hesitated only an instant before dislocating the hip, incising the face, the eyes, the genitals, having learned to use humor as an effective defense mechanism. The more disgusting the task—the closer we came to losing our precious objectivity—the more bawdy and raucous the lab sessions. Male genitalia, for example, would invariably end up in an unsuspecting student's knapsack or pocket. A dehumanizing and shameful way of coping, but a way of coping nonetheless.

We saw anatomy through to the bitter and ludicrous end. By then the forms were almost unrecognizable. Some had commenced decomposition and were practically unbearable to be near. We had dislocated joints, amputated limbs, split the skull, bisected the head—making use of not only scalpels and fingers, but handsaws, electric saws, mallets and chisels, all according to directions in the tattered, greasy, dog-eared lab manual. It was degrading past the point of absurdity. At no small cost, desensitization had been achieved.

"You're in medical school? Very good. I always wanted to be a doctor, but I just wasn't cut out for it. Did you have to work on cadavers?"

"Sure."

He shrugs heroically.

# Sick at Heart

## by Susan Chiarrello

Johnny looked barely nineteen, his face young and bewildered beneath his corn rows. In his white hospital gown his dark skin had a sallow cast, and the skin on his thin arms looked dry and scaly. When I entered his isolation room he jerked his head in my direction.

"What ch'all fixin' to do to me today?"

"I'm your student nurse today, Johnny."

"Yeah? You're number six. Who else gets a crack at me?"

"Whoever can help you better."

He lifted himself slowly in the bed. "Let's get one thing straight, student nurse number six. I have been here six weeks already and y'all have worn me out. A different person walks in this room every hour with something he's gonna do for me. I need rest. Get that right, and you and me'll get along fine."

I nodded nervously, having read his medical history. In six weeks the residents, who rotated monthly, had suggested at least six different diagnoses, beginning with endocarditis, or heart inflammation, and including cancer, tuberculosis, and lung abscesses. He had endured painful procedures, such as bone marrow aspiration, thoracentesis, lung scans, brain scans, and echocardiograms, often within hours of one another. Despite these tests, he did not improve, losing weight daily, continuing to run a fever, and developing a hacking cough and continuous diarrhea.

"But Johnny, we have to do these things to get you well."

"You let me rest, girl, I'll get well." His thin face broke into a wide smile. "I'm a survivor."

When I entered his room again a half hour later, a doctor stood over Johnny's bed. Next to him lay a mess of needles, alcohol swabs, and blood-soaked four-by-fours.

---

*Susan Chiarrello is a pseudonym for a nurse who works in a San Francisco bay area hospital. All names in her story have been changed.*

"Nothing to it, Johnny," he was saying. He bent over Johnny with a long silver needle. "One slow prick...then a burning sensation."

Johnny groaned.

"That's it, John. All there is to it."

"You through yet?" Johnny gasped.

"Damn it! All I get is fluid." The doctor poked Johnny five more times before he gave up, throwing down his needles in frustration. Johnny lay there moaning as the doctor, disgusted, walked out the door, leaving his bloodied equipment tangled among the sheets.

The cardiology resident, Mitch Robbins, walked in 15 minutes later accompanied by a group of interns and residents.

"Hi there, Johnny! How's it going?" Robbins exclaimed brightly.

"How d'ya think, when I get stabbed six times before breakfast?"

Robbins laughed, then pushed Johnny forward in the bed. He listened to Johnny's chest intently through his stethoscope. In a moment he flashed a significant look at the others.

"Hey, listen to this."

Johnny had seen his look. "What ch'all hear?"

"A little sound in your heart, Johnny, that's all."

"What's it mean?"

"Nothing, Johnny. Just leave the problem solving to us."

I followed the doctors into the hall. They stood in a small circle, talking in lowered voices.

"A heart murmur, clear as a bell," Robbins was saying. "He needs a heart catheterization immediately. This spells endocarditis for sure."

"Yeah, a damn shame we took him off antibiotics."

Robbins went back in and asked Johnny to sign a consent form for the somewhat risky heart catheterization. At the mention of another test Johnny looked up sharply. "Y'all don't know what's wrong with me yet? What ch'all been doing for the last six weeks?"

"We have an idea, but we need proof. Just sign here."

"Naw!" With painful effort Johnny hoisted himself to a sitting position. "Y'all don't know now, you never will. I need rest, and I ain't signing."

Robbins turned and grabbed my arm, propelling me out of the room in front of him. "He doesn't know what he's saying. Get some Valium ready, and go get Rogers. He's probably talking to some patient."

I found Greg Rogers, a young resident, talking to an old Filipino woman. He was tall and thin, with a soft Afro that stood out like a cloud around his expressive face.

"Mitch Robbins wants you to talk to Johnny Green. He's refusing a heart catheterization. Robbins suggested Valium."

"A unique way to obtain consent, isn't it?" He turned back to his patient. "Excuse me, Mrs. Sanchez, my fans are calling."

I followed him out to the nurses' station, where Robbins was writing on Johnny's chart.

"It's got to be done, Rogers," Robbins said immediately. "We heard a murmur this morning."

"I diagnosed endocarditis six weeks ago. You told me then I was wrong."

"Damn it, Rogers, the blood cultures were negative. And keep your voice down."

"If we had kept him on those same antibiotics, he might never have developed this murmur," said Rogers.

"We don't know that for sure. And it's the last thing you want someone to overhear," said Robbins.

Rogers' hands were in tight fists at his sides.

"Just get him to sign the consent," Robbins insisted. "Call him 'brother' if that'll work, but don't come out of that room without the consent signed. Then we'll have our diagnosis, and we won't have to sweat it." Rogers stared at him for a long time, the skin over his high cheekbones a deep maroon. Then he picked up the syringe that was lying on the desk in front of him and headed for Johnny's room.

When I entered, Rogers was drawing a diagram while Johnny looked on in horrified fascination.

"That stuff is growing in my heart?"

"If you've ever shot up, the germs in your blood can get stopped on the heart valves. If the germs grow too long, we hear a murmur. That's what they heard in your heart this morning," said Rogers.

"What happens to me if I have this test?" Johnny asked, his voice quavering.

"Possible problems—blood clots, infections. But there's a much bigger risk if we don't."

"If you promise me no more tests but this one, then go to it," Johnny sighed, leaning back on the pillow. "I can't seem to fight you all, noways nohow."

Rogers stood up and let out a deep breath, his hand shaking slightly as he handed Johnny the consent form and a pen. We both watched Johnny scrawl his signature with an unsteady hand.

I spent the rest of that day cleaning Johnny of his diarrhea, sponging him for his high temperature, suctioning him of the thick mucus in his chest. Between these procedures Johnny told me about himself.

He hadn't shot drugs for a long time. He had worked for several years at a gas station, but he had to leave when a black man held up the place and the owners assumed Johnny was involved. "I was mad as hell. So I started hustling," he said.

Then he worked in a boiler factory for a couple of years, and during this time he went with a woman. When he was laid off she left him. "Didn't seem to matter much what I did after that."

I asked him why she split. He looked at me like I was crazy and asked me how many women I knew who would put up with a man with no job and no money in a hole like East Oakland. I asked him what he would do when he got out of the hospital, and he shrugged his thin shoulders.

"Girl, I'd cry, I think. I'd laugh. But after that...all I know is them streets."

At one the next afternoon I pushed Johnny out of the elevator and into the shadowy corridors of the surgical floor.

Johnny rapidly turned his head from side to side.

"What is this place?" he yelled.

"It's the surgery floor, Johnny."

"This place ain't no damn surgery. This place is a morgue. They bring people here to die. You hear me? I ain't staying."

The corridors echoed with a page for Rogers. Johnny's hands gripped the rails of the gurney as Rogers scurried toward us down the long hall, carrying a syringe. He leaned over the gurney, speaking rapidly.

"Johnny, it's almost over. I'll come up and talk to you when it's through," said Rogers.

"This place is spooky, man! It smells like death, man!"

"It's the basement, that's all. I'm just going to give you a drug to help you through this."

Rogers pierced Johnny's I.V. with a syringe of Valium, then nodded for me to wheel him into the operating room.

Back in his room two hours later, Johnny lay back exhausted in his bed.

"I don't trust these motherfuckers an inch," he told me. "And I'm sicka not knowing what they be doing to me."

"What do you understand?" I asked.

"I know I shot up with dirty needles, fucked up my heart. I know I need rest, and these motherfuckers ain't giving me a chance in hell to get it. And I know I can't fight them."

"You fight them pretty well, Johnny."

"Yeah? You noticing me winning any of these fights?"

Later I saw Rogers go in to talk to Johnny at his bedside. He told Johnny that they had found vegetation growing on his heart valves and that he would probably need surgery. As I stood in the doorway, Johnny sent me another long, despairing look. Then he pulled the sheet over his head, as if to shut us all out.

I met Mitch Robbins coming up in the elevator the next Monday morning.

"Heard about Johnny Green? Had a respiratory arrest on Friday," he said.

"Is he alive?" I asked. I felt stunned.

"He's in intensive care. But he's done for."

"What happened?"

He shrugged as the elevator doors opened. "Who knows?" We might have dislodged some vegetation when we did the heart cath. The guy was in terrible shape, anyway."

I walked into the intensive care unit and saw Johnny lying to my right. He had cotton restraints on his wrists and bandages over his eyes. Lights were blinking, and monitors were giving off their warning buzzes. When a machine buzzed he would twist his head from left to right, right to left, as though he were trying, even now, to understand and do battle with those forces overpowering him.

"Johnny, take it easy. Try to rest now," I said. His head

stopped turning for a second, and I remembered the old Johnny, straining intently to listen and comprehend.

"No hope for that one. Those are purposeless head movements," a blonde nurse said coolly.

"Take good care of him. He was a wonderful guy," I said.

She stared at me in disbelief. "An addict, wasn't he?" she said.

# A Sunday Afternoon of Blood and Pain

*by George H. Lewis*

It is a warm Sunday afternoon, and the sun has pushed back the swollen rain clouds that clustered over Stockton for most of the past week. Cheryl and I walk, smelling the incredible fragrance of trees and flowers in bloom that floats over the city in spring. It has been a busy week.

"Which car should I take?"

"The Cruiser, of course," I say, patting its golden fender as I go around to open the door. "Should we take Pacific Avenue?"

"No, let's go up Pershing. We'll see more trees in bloom."

"Pershing it is." I wheel the Cruiser into traffic and adjust the volume control on the radio to a comfortable level. The Cruiser allows only KRAK to be played on its radio. Country music hums softly in the background.

"We've been really lucky with the Cruiser," Cheryl says.

"How so?"

"Hardly any repairs since we borrowed it from your Dad. Rides well. Gets pretty good mileage. Not bad for a 1970 Plymouth."

"Not bad at all," I agree, shifting into the outside lane of traffic to cross March Lane.

Then there is a blur in my left eye and something smashes my shoulder. Hard.

We are floating. Why is Cheryl pushed up between the dash and the steering wheel, looking at me that way?

The Cruiser shudders and stops. So does time. Cheryl and I look at each other.

"Are you hurt?"

"I don't think so." I can see blood staining her blonde hair. Like in a film that has stopped, and suddenly begun again, I

---

*George H. Lewis teaches sociology at the University of the Pacific in Stockton, California.*

begin to see beyond her eyes, to hear the screams around us.

Smoke drifts back from the sadly crumbled nose of the Cruiser. I twist the ignition key. It is jammed on. I try to reach across Cheryl and open the door. Strange faces peer in the windows.

Where is my strength? I wonder. I move like a deep-sea diver, clumsy and slow. The scream of tearing metal, already a memory, is just beginning to penetrate. I must be careful not to hurt Cheryl. I lean over to push on the door.

Someone is asking me something. I see a strange bearded face close to mine. I nearly fall. Cheryl is sitting near a lamp post. Some people are talking to her.

Sixty yards down the road there is a mound of dirt and yellowish metal. It looks like a bulldozer in a construction site. Only it is on its side. There are a lot of people around it.

Everything is out of focus. I feel my head. My glasses are gone. Of course.

"My glasses are gone," I tell the bearded face.

"I think you'd better sit down, too. You look pretty pale."

We walk toward the side of the road. The light changes and cars accelerate around us. The noise seems very loud. My ankle begins to hurt. Later I will find out it is broken.

The face of a friend. "My God, George, are you all right?"

"I think so." Why can't I ever think of something clever to say when I need to?

"He was going very fast. After he hit you, he rolled over two or three times. He hit several more cars. The police say he hit me, too, but I'm not sure."

"Is that him?" I point toward the strange bulldozer with the people around it.

"Yes."

"How is he?"

The beard answers. "No one knows. I think there are a couple dead down there. His whole car smells like a brewery."

Paramedics are checking Cheryl. She is having trouble breathing. The whole area stinks of oil and exhaust. Every time the light changes, there is more. You can feel it move over you, like wind.

I sit down and wipe some grit from the corner of my eye. It is in my teeth, too. I look at my hand. It sparkles. The grit is glass, crushed fine as sand.

A woman is talking to Cheryl. She is talking too fast. I can't seem to follow.

"...came through the red light straight at us...swerved into you...my husband screamed..."

She holds a little boy by his hand. His eyes are looking far off and not at us. He is shaking all over, like he is very cold. He never speaks.

I walk back to the Cruiser, talking to a policeman. He has sketched a four-way intersection on a gray piece of paper. He keeps getting the wrong page in his notebook. I think he is doing a good job. He is polite and gentle. I want to find my glasses. I never do.

The Cruiser looks very strange. There is no front fender on my side of the car, where I patted it just minutes before we hopped in. The hood is crumpled and nearly gone. The engine seems twisted and broken. It is steaming slowly. The wheels are bent in. In front of the windshield, there is very little of my car to recognize.

There is a third person in the ambulance with us. He is wearing a gray checked flannel shirt and smells like cheap rum. There is a gauze bandage around his head. It is leaking red into his hair.

"What happened, man? Who hit me?" he says. The medic tries to get his name and address. He turns to Cheryl.

"Do you know what's goin' on here, babe? Somebody run a red light?"

She moves closer to me. Her face is very pale. I look at my hand, holding hers. My finger is bleeding, where the edge of my wedding ring has cut it open.

"What the hell is goin' on? This isn't real."

At the hospital we wait. Three ambulances have come in at once. There are no beds left.

"Sunday afternoons are always bad," an orderly says.

Cheryl is finally given a bed near Gray Checked Shirt. He refuses to give names or phone numbers of relatives. He refuses to take a blood test.

"It's the law," the doctor says.

"Whose law? Not mine!"

"We'll force you to take the test if you don't cooperate."

"Well, man, it's not any law I ever heard of."

I am wheeled into X-ray. The technician apologizes for the delay.

"The guy before you was smashed up real bad. He kept moving around and screaming. We just got to wipe the blood off the table before you got on."

As we leave the hospital, we hear a nurse and the doctor talking about Gray Checked Shirt in another room.

"He's gone."

"Who?"

"The driver. He must have just got up and walked out."

"Well, he's drunk, he's probably got a concussion, and he does have a pretty big hole in his head. But it's not my problem."

At home in bed we lie and look at each other. We have slowly gone over each other's body, washing cuts and stroking bruises.

"We're like two monkeys, picking off lice."

"Hey..."

"Yeah?"

"Want a sandwich?"

"Can you get it on your crutches?"

"Sure. No problem."

Later, we try to make love. But we are too sore. That's funny but we are also too sore to laugh.

# Higher Education
*by Lauren Trownsell*

People who drink in the afternoon are different from those who drink at night. The day drinkers usually wander in alone, hoping to find a friend playing pinball, a good number to bet, or a blonde, 18-year-old preppie-cum-barmaid, working the day shift after her morning classes. You could cash your unemployment check in my register, bet some numbers, and drink the rest away in my bar.

"Life's a bitch," you tell me, and I ask you, "One more time, Hon?" until the wife sends in the kid to fish you out. But it's funny—each time the kid comes in, he sees the pinball machines, all lit up with pictures of harem girls, cowgirls, supergirls, all with swollen breasts.

"Daddy, can I have a quarter for the machine?" He plays the game and watches the tits light up as the silver ball hits the 1000 hole. Those girls don't look like Mommy outside in her curlers. Daddy makes time for another shot.

I never got around to feeling sorry for the wives standing outside the bar, waiting with an armful of groceries, waiting for their men to come out. After all, they had waited all through grammar school to marry these men, waited less than nine months to start a family, waited constantly for their men to come home. They were used to waiting.

I had waited for things, too. But not the same things. I had no affinity with these waiting women. I had waited for a raise or for my heavy hitters to come in and decorate the bar with 10 spots. Or for a time when the place might be empty—I could pull out my French book and memorize the Perfect Past. But usually I just waited for the fourth Bloody Mary to go to my head.

---

*This story is from the "Other Voices" column—a reader-written one—from the* Village Voice. *The last the* Voice *knew, Lauren Trownsell had left for Hong Kong.*

The fun would start when Georgie walked in around three o'clock. Georgie was the resident bookie, "the man with the sheets." He would pull out his numbers sheets and spread them out on the bar near the pay phones. Then he'd put on his glasses and order a "Black-on-the-rocks-splash-of-soda," for which he never paid. Georgie was a preferred customer. He'd look through his papers, occasionally muttering, "Oh shit."

By 3:30 the operation was well under way. The phone on the wall would start ringing, and two boys, 12 years old, would come in the side door. Sometimes they still had their school books with them, and they always had "the envelopes." Mickey and Carmine were runners. While school friends were out shooting baskets, these two were making $10 a day delivering the sheets and collecting "the envelopes."

Mickey and Carmine, despite their profession, were average 12-year-olds. They dreamed of Camaros when they couldn't afford bicycles. Hard liquor still tasted funny to them, but beer they could handle. And their first White Russians went so smoothly that they discovered a quick one before their "errands" was more fun than stopping at 7-11 for slurpees.

They, too, liked to watch the girls on the pinball machines. A pair of neon tits was healthy reward for hitting the 1000 hole. But one game was all they had time for before Georgie was ready to send them running with a few copies of the *Argus* under their arms to look like paper boys.

Like a young Greenwich mother waving her kids off to day camp, I watched Mickey and Carmine slide out the door, into the street. I could almost hear myself telling them to button their coats, avoid puddles, or "Don't talk to strangers." But oh, the things kids learn at day camps! I couldn't help worrying about them. The boys made me vulnerable again, for I hadn't worried about anyone in a long time. They were the darlings who loved me and tortured me and convinced me never to have children of my own. "Darlings" really do turn into derelicts and drunks.

Back in the bar an hour later, the boys looked so cocky. They were 12, running numbers, drinking White Russians, and they could talk about a woman's breasts. But if they weren't home by 6:30 sharp Mom wasn't gonna wait dinner any longer.

Mickey, Carmine, and I had more in common than we

could ever admit. We were all fronts—willing ones—for an operation we knew little about. We didn't know how much money we were standing on, or that our cut was a fraction of the percentage usually allotted to "innies." We didn't know that the cops knew and we didn't know that down in the Bronx, D.A. Merola was banging his head against a wall.

But we did know some things, we learned from each other. We knew that you could buy the best Mexican stilettos in a store on 231st Street, and we knew who to ask for when you went into the store. We knew that if you wanted a lot of quick cash, you could call the DeAntonio brothers at 15 percent a day. We knew that if you wanted a passport, driver's license, or government service I.D., Sonny on Marshall Avenue could have it for you the next day with $100 down. We knew that ugly girls could get pregnant and ugly men could get very ugly.

Yes, I worried about Mickey and Carmine, but I couldn't feel sorry for them. In fact, they had it good. They had a jump start on things. I who had spent my youth dreaming of becoming a dancer, of becoming a lady, only to end up pouring liquor for those who once had dreams as well. Mickey and Carmine, they were already the "not for nothing" boys. They could smell a rat for miles. They had absorbed so much and knew so little; and I was right behind them.

Mickey and Carmine are 14 now and they don't run numbers anymore. But I saw them a couple of weeks ago at an after-hours club down on Bainbridge Avenue near the elevated tracks. They said hello and asked me how I was protecting myself these days. I told them I talk good and still pack a stiletto. Mickey said a blade won't stop a bullet, and if I was interested he'd show me a little .38 that wouldn't knock my shoulder out of joint.

"Don't tell me you're running guns now, you guys," I said, a little too loud for an after-hours club. "Who are you running for?"

But that information was not privy to me. Carmine shot me a look that told me I should know better than to ask. "Just making talk," I choked.

It wasn't the same anymore. They had learned how to drink Wild Turkey and they had learned how not to talk. They had learned how to get a bigger cut out of a smaller operation.

They had learned where to go to suck the breasts of wild pinball women. "Suck or be sucked," Georgie had once said. And they had learned that people should always be viewed as transient, that just because we were in the same numbers game two years ago was no reason to trust me till I had put my money down and taken the gun.

I went out to the garage in back and took target practice on the wall. Just like Mickey promised, it didn't take my shoulder off. The boys were good businessmen.

Yes, they knew their trade well. And me? I need to be getting home now. I keep forgetting I'm a college student, whatever that means. I think it means I have a class at 10:30, and that I have to read *David Copperfield* by May.

I'm working another bar now where I only keep the .38 with me on weekends. And if anybody's looking to buy a good stiletto that only went through one Puerto Rican in two years—I could use the cash—I'll let it go for cheap.

# City Streets: Three Stories from a Policeman's Notebook
*by Bob Rogers*

*It had been too hot for too many days.* Nights brought no relief—only a steaming darkness through which frantic sounds were magnified in a disorder of public and private noise. Someone yelled; a car screeched out of the projects; a toilet flushed loudly amidst the rattle of sweaty, drunken laughter; the urgency of the 11 o'clock news blared from a blue-lit room.

Jess and I had been patrolling the streets for about 10 minutes, trying to adjust to the heat-induced swirl of activity—the car's squawking radio, the whir of street noise, the flux of movement in your gut—which, after days off with family and friends, displaces whatever state you've come to duty in. When you're lucky, you adjust quickly to the frightening present.

The initial call was broadcast as a possible overdose. We responded and went to the apartment. There was that familiar smell, which becomes *the* smell—that stench of poorly ventilated rooms occupied by too many people and too much sorrow. It was easier to think of it that way than to deal with the searingly frightening knowledge that it probably was instead some stink of evil upon anger upon hope.

An old black man was sitting on a rickety wooden chair, his yellowed shirt catching the tears that dropped onto his heaving chest. The girl—I can't remember her name either—was lying very still on the floor between us. We began—but soon gave up—looking for signs of life.

After shaking his head several times, the man looked towards us. "She's real sick this time, officer. It's that damned dope that did it." We could hear the ambulance siren, but it was too late. She was dead.

"I'm her grandfather, officer. This here lady is her aunty.

---

*Bob Rogers is a San Francisco policeman.*

We takes care of those children for her."

The two boys in polo shirts and underwear were five or six. They had brushed by their mother and stepped over her once already. The smaller one played peek-a-boo over the man's leg while the other ate from a cereal box. The younger boy climbed onto his lap, seeking a safe place in the old man's arms, which moved to brace him so he wouldn't fall. The boy with the cereal box looked at his mother, then at us, then ran to another room. The little one slid off the old man's lap and hop-skipped after his brother.

The ambulance crew moved past us, knelt down only briefly and then turned to us, giving us the look. There's a way we shrug, shake our heads or grimace that is the real pronouncement of death, and it's probably those pained, embarrassed or insulated looks that the family will remember us by. We know that afterwards we will retreat to paper work and procedural routine—distractions which get us through those times that we wish were not a part of our job.

"Did you guys call the coroner yet?" We hadn't.

The woman moved rigidly from one doorway to another, folding her thin rope-cord arms and glaring at the girl on the floor. Her voice was hard and sharp as she snarled about the pimp that had hooked this child. She gave us details for our report, adding bits of information which completed the picture of despair. She busied herself in tense, quick movements, picking up, folding, unfolding and refolding again whatever was before her. She took the old man his heart pills and yelled that he must take some—her voice becoming louder as her tears flowed faster.

The dead girl, from the signs that scarred her body, had been on heroin and probably a carnival of other street junk that poisons so many in the ghetto. At that time I'm not sure whether I had stopped wondering about the dead and what hopes and feelings they might have carried. This girl had no future and it no longer mattered how terrible her past might have been. Dead was dead.

The ambulance crew left and we waited with the three of them in the living room. My partner was better at handling their grief than I, listening and talking to them sympathetically, encouragingly, while I worked on a clipboard of official forms.

I stood awkwardly, writing amidst their pain—not sure how to say how sorry I was.

The coroner came and went, leaving us alone. The man told us that the girl's mother had run off somewhere, leaving her daughter for them to raise. They had tried, he said, but she was just too wild. When she was in her early teens, she had gotten pregnant, and then a year or two later—by this time hooked and lost on drugs—she had had the second child. He said he must have done something wrong and began crying again. Jess put his hand on the old man's shoulder, allowing his grief to flow, pausing before giving him reassurance.

The woman began calling relatives, and after what we felt was a decent interval we said goodnight and wished them luck.

Back in the patrol car, each alone with our thoughts... We always worry most about the kids and I hoped that, after this, life would have some breaks for these children. There was always that chance that luck, love, care and whatever else it took would make life more than it had been for their mother. Whenever I thought it impossible, I remember that my partner had made it from a neighborhood just like this one.

We went back several months later intending to visit them, but they were gone—some Housing Authority move, probably—and the new tenant didn't know their new address.

I never saw them again, but the scene seems forever to be repeating itself—only with different lives and different deaths.

*A transitional neighborhood—that's one thing you could call it.* The kind of place where you could buy a decaying Victorian cheaply, resurrect it, realize a profit and then, hopefully, be gone before you learn too much about rage and violence.

We got the call on the radio as "Man down—possible gunshot victim." As soon as we saw him we knew he was dead. The blood was too thick, the face too gray. He might have been 20. From the clothing and very short hair, we figured he was from the Zen Buddhist Center a block away.

We started the police stuff—securing the scene, notifying the lab, Homicide, and our sergeant. I had some tape and used it to rope off the area around him. Other units arrived, and then the press and bystanders. Noise welled up around his stillness.

The Buddhist priests, monks, and students stood quietly behind the cordoned-off area and watched the official activity.

We cops sometimes forget those who are grieving—we talk casually, go from task to task busily, and the dead lie on the stone cold street. I tried to understand what the Buddhists were thinking and feeling as they stood there in the street-lit night, the spinning lights of the different official cars sweeping across their very quiet faces.

It was a robbery, we guessed, but there were no witnesses. In this neighborhood there were always victims. Some were there in the housing projects, languishing and festering. I guess someone could make some sociological sense out of this, but nothing will ever be as real as the cold body on the street, or the horror-bound soul who did this thing and waits for his own brutal end.

*It was Easter Sunday dawn.* We had worked since 10 the night before on the streets downtown. Suspects, victims, witnesses, punks—a montage of movement herky-jerked in our tired minds; memories trying to die. The streets were quiet now.

Jess and I were sitting in the car, the breaking sun burning into our brains. We were tired—we were always tired. Jess rarely slept well, and I never seemed to sleep enough either to rid myself of that gnawing ache I could not name that lingered and held on until the whirl of work at midnight distracted me.

We were spending the few minutes before sign-off time just thinking of something to say to each other. We liked each other a lot, but were perhaps too much alike to be spontaneous. So much was always left unsaid.

I saw the guy approaching from the rear of the patrol car. As I sat there, I unsnapped my holster and held the gun alongside my leg, aware that I was now doing all of the precautionary things I had once thought were just for the macho and the paranoid. The man stopped at my window, looking like any man about to ask directions.

"I want to turn myself in," he said.

These episodes almost always end with some loosely-wrapped, frightened soul thanking you for your canned speech, shaking your hand and then walking away until the next series of circumstances becomes too much for him. Cops develop this method of interaction which keeps the jails from getting clogged with these poor creatures the psych wards cannot accept. If you can calm them down it often keeps them out of trouble—which is, too, a way of keeping yourself out of it as well.

I tried to suppress a here-we-go-again look to Jess and asked the man what was wrong. "I've killed somebody," he said, looking first at me and then at my partner.

"Come on, pal, relax. What makes you think you killed somebody?" This is the point where they usually give us the business about people turning into snakes and crawling through faucets or of mothers making their children eat live rats.

"Please come, he's in my room. It's right around the corner." Looking at him, seeing him, we knew we'd have to check it out.

We walked with him to the decaying hotel and went upstairs to his room. We stood in the hall waiting for him to find his key. I thought of the police officer recruitment campaigns which offer applicants an opportunity to be in a "service" oriented profession; the notions we all probably had about the excitement and "never a dull moment" dimension. After five years as a cop I'd had thousands of experiences and non-tedious moments, and yet, for the most part, life seemed to wind through the grimness of standing in hallways, getting through your shift and away from the dreadful sameness. We told the nervous man to relax. More and more you become less in a hurry.

He opened the door. There was the body on the bed. The throat was bruised and the legs were jutting stiffly over the edge of the bed.

The tiny room was neither bright nor dark. The attempts of early morning sunlight to penetrate it were futile against the oily parchment window shade and blue-green plastic curtains. The room was afoul in a grimness which seemed to emit its own light. The mottled blue and gray body did not seem so out of place upon the soiled bare mattress in that dirty lifeless place. There were no chairs and only a chipped and gouged chest. The rug was blackened with cigarette burns and littered with assorted filth. Two or three squat candles stuck in saucers must have served at night to illuminate this dreary place.

We tied up all the procedural requirements and took the man to be booked. The narrative in his statement basically said that he had been angry at his lover and wanted to send him to Heaven on Easter morning. "Did he lose his best friend?" another cop passing through the booking area asked. Unfazed now, our man's concern was that he be allowed to call someone to pass on the message that he would not be in to work on Monday.

We left work late that morning. I'm not sure how Jess slept that day, but that lingering ache I was unable to describe the day before interfered with the sound sleep I craved.

# Verdict for a Bathtub Killing: A Juror's Testimony

*by Barbara Lee*

I considered myself lucky—my first summons for jury duty and I was assigned to a murder case. The myth held by my fellow scientists is that people like us were routinely rejected by the prosecution—we are too analytical, too soft, and too likely to overlook the defendant's crimes in the context of society's ills. But now I sit in the jury box, one of the 12— 5 men and 7 women—selected from more than 100 potential jurors. Some automatically declined to sit in on a murder trial; others who are closely connected with law officers or have themselves suffered from violent crimes have been excused. A few are too vague or disorganized to satisfy either the defense or the prosecution. One man said he felt being confined in a jury room would arouse his claustrophobia.

The 12 of us who survived the extensive questioning are almost entirely middle-class—professionals, executives, housewives.

The assistant district attorney outlines the alleged crime in his opening statement. The defendant, Kenneth "Bo" Bodie, has been charged with the felony murder of James McCreary— that is, with participating in a robbery during the course of which the victim was killed. According to the prosecutor's scenario, Shirley Murray casually dropped into McCreary's Harlem apartment a few blocks away from hers at 1:00 a.m. one night. Leaving to buy some beer with $10 he had given her, she ran into her boyfriend, Willie Foy, and the defendant. (We are told that Bodie and his girlfriend shared an apartment with Murray and Foy.) The two men forced her to return

---

*This story is from* Harper's Weekly, *published from late 1974 to early 1976, which featured reader-written articles. At that time Barbara Lee lived in New York City. Neither* Harper's Magazine *nor this editor knows where she is today.*

with them to McCreary's apartment, where they robbed him, tied him up and then dragged him into the bathroom and plunged him into a scalding hot bath.

Murray then ran back to her apartment and called the police, who found McCreary, badly burned, in his home and took him to the hospital. Bodie and Foy had already left McCreary's place, stealing his cameras and sports jackets, which they brought to their apartment.

Afterwards, Bodie went to a hospital for treatment of the burns he had received when he pushed McCreary into the tub. Two days later, McCreary died, and the police picked up Murray. She eventually disclosed the identity of the two men.

The victim was a 26-year-old black government worker. The other three parties are also black but unemployed.

The defense lawyer does not present an alternative scenario. We are simply reminded that the burden of proof rests with the prosecution.

The first day's witnesses describe in detail the circumstances of the crime. We are shown the carefully drawn diagrams of McCreary's apartment, and photographs, from every angle, of the scene of the crime. Evidently, Willie Foy has already been tried—almost every exhibit has a scratch-out number on the back from a previous trial—but it is clear that we will not be informed of the outcome of his case.

Movie and television courtroom dramas I have watched have not prepared me for the endless delays, the constant waiting—waiting in the jury room till the courtroom is somehow prepared for our arrival; waiting in the jury box as defense counsel and prosecution, huddling around the judge's bench, discuss the latest objection. The defense objects to the inclusion of every piece of evidence. In the face of these continual, sometimes acrimonious, objections, mostly denied, the judge remains even-tempered.

On the second day, Murray is in the witness box. She is 19, small but voluptuous, dressed in a tight skirt and a low-cut white blouse. A gold cross rests in her emphatic cleavage. She is deadpan in her recital of her story of the crime and its aftermath, and it is obvious that her strange behavior—why, for example, she called the police if she was unwilling to name the alleged perpetrators immediately—will never be explained under the rigid rules of questioning.

Murray's words are slurred and mumbled. Her account is continually interrupted by requests from the defense to have her testimony read back by the court stenographer. I can't help wondering whether she told this same story at Foy's trial. Did she show greater emotion then?

At one point Murray claims that "Niggers like that (Bodie) should be got off the street." One of the defense lawyers, a suave, well-dressed young black pounces on the remark. She modifies it to "people like that," but is finally forced to retrieve her original words. On cross examination, the defense persistently tries to suggest that she has rehearsed her story with the D.A.

Other witnesses fill in the details in the course of the week: mother of the victim identifies as her son's jacket the one Foy was wearing when he was arrested; the detective who investigated the murder reports in precise detail a year-old event (but he is unable to remember at what time he had lunch two days ago); a fingerprint expert identifies some of the fingerprints found in the victim's apartment as matching those of Willie Foy; a records supervisor from a hospital testifies that she has located a medical form stating that a "Lyman" Bodie was treated for burns on the night of the crime (the birthday is the same as Kenneth Bodie's, but the address is fictional); and, from the same hospital, a weary-looking doctor says he treated Lyman Bodie's burns, and is surprised to be asked whether he can identify the defendant from the hundreds of cases that must regularly pass through his hands. Finally, the medical examiner takes the stand and describes in clinical detail the effects of the second- and third-degree burns that covered 70 percent of McCreary's body.

The defense presents no witnesses. Their summation provides us with no alternate scenarios. The entire defense rests on the claim that Shirley Murray is a liar. Now we are listening to the judge, who explains clearly how the law should guide us, defining a "reasonable doubt" as a doubt based on reason, not emotion or prejudice, and pointing out that to be guilty of felony murder, one need only be a participant in the crime, not in the murder itself.

Finally, we are sent to the jury room to deliberate. The

constraint of listening to the proceedings is ended, and we are free to talk about what has been absorbing us for the past week. After an initial burst of discussion, we set up a procedure. We will have a preliminary vote; each person will explain the reasons for his or her position when recognized by Sara, the forewoman, a hefty black practical nurse. (As the first juror selected, Sara automatically became forewoman.)

The initial vote is six guilty, four undecided, and two not guilty. I am one of the undecided, reluctant to vote guilty until I have satisfied myself that there is no alternative.

As we discuss the reasons for our votes, it becomes clear that no one fully believes Murray. We could easily convict on the basis of the fingerprints and the jacket if we were trying Willie Foy, but Bodie, the sullen, depressed young defendant, whose voice we have never heard, is linked to the crime only by Murray's testimony and one flimsy piece of paper, the hospital burn record.

We break for dinner and are marched to a nearby Italian restaurant by good-natured guards. The two alternates sit at another table, confined to each other's company, not allowed to deliberate with, or even talk to, the regular jurors.

Back in the jury room, we decide to have all of Murray's testimony read back to us in an attempt to answer some of the questions that have arisen about it. This resolves some points, but also raises other questions.

Could Murray and her boyfriend have done it themselves? No, the victim was too big a man for fewer than two men to have held him down in the tub. And if Murray had participated in the crime, why would she then call the police? Most incriminating is the burn record of someone who gave the same last name and birthdate as the defendant, but a nonexistent address.

We analyze over and over again all possible explanations for these facts, even chasing down the possibility that someone, maybe Willie Foy, has attempted to incriminate Bodie. The judge instructed us not to consider the failure to present a defense as any evidence of guilt, and we scrupulously observe this direction, though we are all puzzled as to why neither the prosecution nor the defense called Foy to the stand.

A few jury members do not participate in the discussion.

They are practically silent. One of them is Sara, who has consistently voted "not guilty." To my surprise, it is the three black members of the jury who are most reluctant to arrive at a verdict of guilty—even though I would have expected them to identify with the victim. Underlying what they say, though never explicitly expressed, is a basic distrust of the police and the district attorney and a suspicion that these forces create their own evidence.

The mood of the jury gradually shifts, as one explanation after another is discarded. When another vote is finally taken, we all vote guilty—except Sara. Her explanation for her vote is passionately expressed: "I ain't never gonna call anybody guilty on the word of that woman. I knows women like her, and she's a liar." Her intensity leaves no room for discussion; we are at an impasse.

We send a note to the judge, describing the 11:1 situation without identifying the juror or the direction of the dissent. The judge calls us in and quietly explains that no other jury will have any more evidence on which to decide than we have. He emphasizes the cost in time and money that another trial would entail.

Wearily we return to the jury room and attempt to discuss the issues of the case with our holdout, but she reiterates again and again the reason for her vote.

By 1:00 a.m., we are no further along, and we notify the judge that we have not yet reached a decision. We are taken to a hotel for the night. En route in the bus, we make one stop at a drugstore to buy toothbrushes.

During this time, a few of us manage to persuade one particularly loud-mouthed young man to stop badgering Sara, since his comments seem only to make her more intransigent. He certainly will not persuade her to change her mind, but who can? The only possibility seems to be Charles, an older, soft-spoken black from the city board of education, who himself has shifted from a not-guilty position.

That night I share a room with Mary, a woman with whom I have become friendly. Too tense to sleep, we lie awake for hours discussing the trial and our fellow jurors. At breakfast in the hotel the next morning, Sara joins our conversation about beds, breakfast preferences and similar trivia; all discussion of the trial is avoided in her presence.

When we return to the jury room, Charles sits near the window with Sara, while the rest of us disperse in small groups around the room, leaving them undisturbed. An hour goes by as the two of them talk; occasionally he moves to the table and takes one of the items of evidence to their private spot near the window.

Slowly, slowly, he takes her through the process the rest of us have gone through, considering and rejecting all the various possibilities. Lunch has already been ordered when they resume their seats at the table, and Charles calls for another vote. The last one to vote is Sara, and I clench my hands, waiting for what she will say. "Guilty." Without coercion or intimidation we have become a unanimous jury.

In the courtroom, the defense requests that the jury be polled. One by one, we answer to our names and repeat the word "guilty." Saying that word is simultaneously an enormous burden and a relief from the intense experience of the trial.

The judge requests us to meet with him in the jury room. He commends us for resolving our differences. Sara beams at his comments. In answer to our questions, he tells us that Willie Foy, who had an extensive criminal record, had been found guilty and is now in prison, a bitter and angry man. I leave the courtroom convinced we have made the right decision.

# Rescue in the South China Sea

*by John Mooney*

We had a pretty unusual day today. Our destroyer spotted a boat in the water, and we rendered assistance. We picked up 65 Vietnamese refugees. It was about a two-hour job getting everyone aboard, and then they had to get screened by Intelligence and checked out by Medical and fed and clothed and all that.

But now they are resting on the hangar deck, and the kids—most of them seem to be kids from what I've seen—are sitting in front of probably the first television set they've ever seen, watching "Star Wars."

Their boat was sinking as we came alongside. They had been at sea five days, and had run out of water. All in all, a couple more days and the kids would have been in pretty bad shape. I guess once in a while we need a jolt like that for us to realize why we do what we do, and how important, really, it can be.

I mean, it took a lot of guts for those parents to make a choice like that—to go to sea in a leaky boat in hope of finding someone to take them from the sea. So much risk! But, apparently, they felt it was worth it rather than live in a Communist country.

For all of our "problems," with the price of gas, and not being able to afford a new car or other creature comforts this year, or our petty harping on our elected officials—who, unfortunately, most of us don't bother to vote for, only bitch about—I really don't see a lot of leaky boats heading out of San Diego looking for the Russian ships out there. And I don't see many of our sailors jumping ship in Hong Kong. We must really have something going for us.

---

*John Mooney, an ordnance man first class, was a member of the VA-56 air wing when it was assigned to the carrier* Midway. *This report was included in a letter to his parents, Mr. and Mrs. Wallace Mooney of Kaukauna, Wisconsin, and appeared in Bill Knutson's column in* The Post-Crescent *published in Appleton. President Reagan learned of the letter and read it as his radio message to the nation on Christmas day 1982.*

The last time I felt this way was on my last visit to Hong Kong, and I went on the train to the Red Chinese border. I saw the guards and the guns and the fence, and I knew it wasn't meant to keep me *out*.

I took some pictures today, but as usual I didn't have the camera with me for the *real* picture—the one blazed in my mind. I had taken about two rolls of film already, and I had just put my camera away and was going across the hangar deck, headed for the compartment. I looked out the aircraft elevator door and saw one of the last trips of many our motor whaleboat made bringing these people to the carrier.

As they approached the ship, they were all waving and trying as best they could to say "Hello, American sailor! Hello freedom man!" It's hard to see a boat full of people like that and not get a lump somewhere between chin and bellybutton. And it really makes one proud and glad to have been lucky enough to be an American.

People were waving and shouting and choking down lumps and trying not to let other brave men see their wet eyes. A lieutenant next to me said, "Yeah, I guess it's payday in more ways than one." (We got paid today.) And I guess no one could really say it better than that.

It reminds us all of what America has always been—a place a man or woman can come to for freedom. I know we're crowded and we have unemployment and we have a real burden with refugees, but I honestly hope and pray we can always find room. We are a unique society, made up of castoffs of all the world's wars and oppressions, and yet we are strong and free. We have one thing in common—no matter where our forefathers came from, we believe in that freedom.

I hope we always have room for one more person, maybe an Afghan or a Pole or someone else looking for a place to rest, where he doesn't have to worry about his family starving or a knock on the door in the night, and where all men who truly seek freedom and honor and respect and dignity for themselves and their posterity can find a place where they can rest and work and finally see their dreams come true and their kids educated and become the next generation's doctors and lawyers and builders and soldiers and sailors.

It's been a real good day. Tomorrow we pull into Singapore

for a well deserved beer and a little rest. We've been out for about a month and we've covered everything from Alaska to Singapore. It's an experience I know I won't forget!

# A Little Boy's Pony
## by Bobby Graham

It had been a week of extra attention, unusual thoughtfulness, and I had so much help around the house that I was baffled. It wasn't that I was an unduly skeptical wife or a disbeliever in everyday human kindness. It was just that for several days Graham had been making coffee in the morning, putting out the trash, and even running errands to the super market without complaining. Then the night the automatic control on the oven went haywire and kept ringing, I figured something was up.

Whenever I got up to attend to the oven control, Graham would say, "No, Honey, don't get up, I'll fix it." Then in another half hour it would go off again and he'd say the same thing. This went on all night! He didn't throw anything or even threaten to sell the apartment house. Was he coming down with the flu? Then, at five o'clock in the morning, when we were lying there very much awake, he said, "Bobby, I have something to tell you."

Had he lost his business? Was he no longer in love with me? A barely audible "Yes" was all I could manage.

"What I want to tell you is this—I'm buying a race horse."

"Buying a what? Do you mean a horse—a horse that runs, runs and wins purses?"

"We hope so, Honey, we hope so."

I lay there thinking that I didn't have a mink coat and we didn't drive a Cadillac. We never wintered in Florida and we didn't own a summer place in Maine. Don't those things usually come before one buys a race horse?

Then I remembered something Graham had told me when we first were married. He was eight years old when he began to petition Santa Claus for a pony. Christmas morning would

---

*Bobby Graham managed her apartment house in Los Angeles from 1965, when this story was written, until her death in 1982.*

arrive along with some substitute for his pony. He would swallow his disappointment and look forward to the next year. This went on until he was 12, when he finally conceded that ponies weren't to be had for the asking.

"What I have in mind is a filly named Lady Erin. She costs only $3500. If she doesn't do well we can breed her and sell her," was what brought me back to the present. All and all it didn't sound too bad.

Christmas was only a few days away and I flew to Texas to spend the holidays with my family, one made up of very proper citizens who read the King James version and *The Wall Street Journal* instead of racing forms! Their savings were invested in tax-exempt bonds and blue-chip stocks instead of fillies who probably won't do well. Stable talk and race track conversation would be as foreign to them as Cantonese.

So, instead, we discussed the children's school activities. We talked about a new piece of real estate Graham had acquired. We cooked the Christmas dinner and talked well into the night. Not one of them mentioned going to the races. I thought it prudent not to introduce Lady Erin.

I returned home New Year's Eve to find that Lady Erin had turned into Parade Light, who cost $5000 and was a gelding. Not only that, he was a three-year-old who had never been to the post and he would cost at least $500 a month. Happy New Year!

Leaving the congested freeway we entered the stable area, which is a little world of its own. In order to enter and belong, one learns a new language, a new way of life. Four o'clock in the morning would find us drinking boiled pot coffee in the tack room. We waited for daylight and the workouts. The days Parade Light went to the post we were up even earlier. Graham wanted plenty of time to rub Parade's legs, all of which was done with the greatest of care. That horse's one ambition seemed to be to take a big bite of Graham! His love for me could have been due to the sugar cubes I sneaked to him when Graham wasn't looking.

Once our horse left for the receiving barn, we would dash over to the track, meeting him again in the saddling paddock. Then we'd watch the parade to the post. I always made it a point to comb my hair, apply fresh lipstick and don my gloves. In case Parade won, I wanted to look just right in the photo of the owners. When the race was over, we'd rush back to the stable to make sure Parade had come through uninjured. Graham would then help "hot walk" him and rub him down. After an hour or so the horse would be cool enough to be placed in his stall.

During this hour trainers, grooms, owners, and hot walkers all stride back and forth in front of the rows of stalls, analyzing why their various horses didn't win: "I told that jock to get him out of the gate and then take holt of him!"... "He let go wide in the stretch"... "He shoulda stayed on the rail."

Finally the talk would turn to the next time out. The condition book listing the races to be run in the next few weeks would be passed around and we'd review entry requirements, type of race, and size of purse. Being a three-year-old, Parade couldn't enter races for the two-year-olds or four-year-olds and up or, naturally, races for fillies only. There was no use looking at the big money stakes either. He wasn't that good! That left us two choices—allowance and claiming races.

In allowance races we would not run the risk of losing him, where in claiming races we would. In a claiming race one agrees to sell his entry to anyone who has a horse at the track for the amount of money listed under the claiming price. That helps keep races honest. A claim can be as high as $20,000 or as low as $3000.

To keep a horse in allowance races he has to be good, given the nature of the competition. So we favored the claiming ones, knowing that Parade couldn't win the big ones and knowing, too, that if we dropped him too low he'd be claimed. Still, the lower we dropped him, the better his chances would be.

How Graham enjoyed the fringe benefits! The sticker on the car that admitted us to the stable area—the free parking in a special place close to the track entrance—the pass book to the club—standing by your horse in the saddling area. All this delighted him.

Parade went to the post twice at Santa Anita. Both times he came in eighth out of twelve. At least he beat four horses! Then Santa Anita was over and we shipped him to Golden Gate in San Francisco. Riley, our trainer, called us the evening he arrived to tell us the track committee was having trouble filling a race the next day and wanted to run Parade. Riley explained that a horse won't run well after being shipped, but if we went along the racing secretary would probably give us a break on something later.

"Go ahead," Graham told him, "but we won't bother about flying up."

"Hold the phone," I yelled, "if he goes to the post, I'm going to be there."

On the flight up Graham sat a little taller in his seat as he held the racing form listing him as owner of Parade Light. Flashing his famous grin he turned to me and said, "Pretty 'tall cotton' for a poor farm boy!"

When we arrived at Golden Gate, Parade looked so perky that I told Graham and Riley I thought he was sure to win. They both explained to me that it was impossible for a horse to win after being shipped, and neither one layed a bet, not even a two-dollar one. I did, though, while they continued to scoff.

As the horses moved to the gate, Riley and I went up to our box and Graham took his movie camera and went closer to the track. Parade broke fourth, moved up to third in the back stretch, and as he rounded the turn he shot out in front by three lengths and stayed there. Parade won it!

I was so excited I kicked off my heels to avoid falling. With shoes in hand, I ran to the Winner's Circle. We posed for the track camera man, and only then did I realize that instead of my shoes being on my feet, they were still clutched tightly in my left hand. But Graham wasn't completely cool either. The shots he took after Parade Light broke to the front were focused on the ground! The last frames show the not so golden Golden Gate dirt.

Parade went to the post 10 times at that track. He got seconds, thirds and fourths, which pay a little, but he didn't come in first again. We brought him back to LA and Hollywood Park, and he was claimed after his first race. We hated to lose him, but we understood the risks and we wished him well.

Three months later we were having another restless night. This time Graham seemed to have indigestion and he complained of a pain in his chest. By the time we were on our way to the hospital, the ache had spread to his arm. As we raced down the freeway he managed to say, "If this is it, remember, we did everything we wanted to... and I had my pony, too."

The week after I could no longer postpone the inevitable. I went to Graham's office to begin to take care of the many details that went with closing a real estate business. None of the papers pertaining to the organization were in order.

Then I picked up a folder labeled "Parade Light." In it was every bill, every receipt, along with a complete accounting including everything, even our dinner at the Top-of-the-Mark the night Parade won. A CPA wouldn't have been more accurate. And then there was the bottom line. The entire five months of owning a race horse had cost us just eight dollars! How glad I am that, finally, Graham had been able to have his pony.

# Just Asking
*by Stephanie Hill*

The funeral was held at her grandmother's church—she was a Seventh Day Adventist. Too hard to believe, but I remember the hard tears I cried after realizing that Yo-Yo was dead.

Now here we were, Yo-Yo and I, seniors at Art and Design High School—I on my way to Cornell and she to Denmark or Sweden or some such exotic place—to be an artist.

"A kidney infection."

So fast—so sudden—and she never gave me back my mother's incense burner (lent secretly). And yes—I was jealous 'cause her green eyes so alive and shapely body always got the boys. Especially the ones I liked (wanted). Remembering—rushing home after the first glimpse of her and combing my hair into the same style.

My mother said I looked like Aunt Sooky.

Yo-Yo looked so bloated in the casket—why did they put that awful orange chiffon mess on her? Her fingers were swollen around the senior class ring—black onyx was the stone she chose.

Yo-Yo!

Stanley, hold me please—I want Yo-Yo!

I grew up in the South Bronx—but my father before me was a dentist. Howard Prep, Fiske, Meharry. I wanted *that*, not five small rooms and fighting into the night—neighbors, brothers, sisters.

Yo-Yo's family were musicians, writers. They lived on Riverside Drive in an apartment on the first floor—we used to knock on the windows for them to buzz us in. Their bohemian ways got to me—like paint on Yo-Yo's foot for three days straight—but her charm and her antique fur coat put away such thoughts. She kissed boys who rode motorcycles.

---

*This story is from the "Other Voices" column—a reader-written one—from the* Village *Voice. Neither the* Voice *nor this editor knows where Stephanie Hill is today.*

High school had been Kahlil Gibran and incense in English Literature and saying "no" to reefers. We read poetry at Cullen Library, and Alexander's banned us from shopping after school 'cause portfolios make such great hiding places.

Yo-Yo! Yolanda Hope Cross.

For a month before she died everyday at lunch she'd ask, "If you got pregnant, would you have the baby?"

Five of us virgins said, "Yes... No... Maybe so... Why, Yo-Yo?"

"I dunno, just asking."

Canned chow mein and noodles on rice and then back to illustration with Mr. Ferguson.

I was in a high school sorority—my other life. I was in the Xinos and Yo-Yo laughed at me for being so dumb. She loved me anyway—I know that 'cause when we went to the TV dance show she made me take off my homemade pink and lace dress and outfitted me in a purple passion velvet pantsuit and black mascara. "Now you look like something."

And she in her African print suit tight across her ass—we flitted onto TV and Jay and the Americans.

And my mother said, "Why'd you change your clothes?—you left here looking like a *lady*!"

Yo-Yo kissed the freedom runners on the George Washington Bridge, a kiss hot enough to last to D.C. (green-eyed passion-flower child).

And we marched in the *Harlem* contingent against the war and she had an Afro first and said that she felt beautiful.

She was *so* beautiful.

And I, a certified intellectually gifted child, was trying so hard to be like her beauty—beautiful.

We both loved Reggie Paige. So-o cute!

Yo-Yo called him from 135th Street and Lenox Avenue and said we were being attacked by a mad pack of blacks—and he came running to the rescue. Boo-hoo.

We went to the Canyou-Act sweatbox and one day he walked me home (remember) and I was scared I knew that my brother would be sweating up a funk and I said good-bye to Reggie on the stoop.

Good-bye, Reggie.

And Yo-Yo, why did I find out from a stranger that you

died from an abortion? Why couldn't I talk to the people who found two quacks to abort you with a dirty hanger and give you gangrene and let your legs be poisoned so that even if you had lived you would have never walked, danced, run through Washington Square again?

Yo-Yo!

When I saw your sister in your coat—why did I want her to go away? Why did I hate the people who cried at your funeral and didn't really love you? (I love you.)

And young and 17 and full of life and laughter––I laughed five minutes after the hearse pulled away, and me and Wynora swore and made a pact not to tell our mothers that you died of an abortion.

And I have a son who owes his life to you, Yo-Yo.

# On Losing a Neighbor

*by Arlene Silverman*

Joanne Miller and her husband and two daughters moved away last week. They moved to the suburbs, leaving me in the space where the moving van had stood, a city dweller waving good-bye as long as I could see the Bekins truck through the fog.

To be honest, this story is really nobody's affair; it is very private business. In fact, Joanne Miller is a made-up name; I thought I'd let her rest peacefully and anonymously with her family in her new home on a Marin hillside. It's one of the last favors I can do for her.

But I will write about Joanne Miller anyway, because she was a *neighbor*, you see—the kind my mother talked about when she told me stories about how people used to be. My mother often mentioned Mrs. Goldstein, who had discovered my brother cowering in a closet when my parents' house caught on fire. She raved about Mrs. Farber, who had gladly shared her electric refrigerator with our family when we were still using the old-fashioned box of ice on the window sill. And she'd sigh every once in awhile as we grew up and say, "Neighbors aren't like that anymore."

Maybe they aren't. There are enough books written and sociological studies touted which say that people just don't care these days. Stories are told again and again of screaming murder victims left to the mercy of their attackers as people peer coldly from behind lace curtains. A friend who has lived in several cities for the sake of her husband's career tells me, "I'm afraid to make friends." Another friend has moved with her husband and the children into a Los Gatos house with another couple because, she says, she wants to provide her

---

*Arlene Silverman is a San Francisco housewife and mother whose impressions have appeared in local publications from time to time. She is, happily, still in touch with her "lost" neighbor.*

children with "family."

When I moved into the quiet, green block on San Francisco's western edge, I must have believed the trends, for I expected little from my new neighbors except, perhaps, a child for my three-year-old daughter to play with and a spot of backyard sunlight for the child that would be born soon after we moved in.

Joanne Miller appeared at my door about a week after we moved in, with a tiny daughter under each arm and a bouquet of flowers in one hand. "Boy, am I glad you've moved in," she said, with a wide no-nonsense smile. "I hear you've got a kid."

At first, it was the children we each saw most. Her tiny, dark-haired beauties would toddle to our door, plugged into bottle or pacifier, or my daughter would be invited to play at the Millers' house. Later, my son would make it a lop-sided foursome.

The hot-line between our houses—there were three quiet, childless homes between us—was busy. One of us would ring the other up: "Gotta run to the store. Can you watch the kids?" Or, simply, "I've got to get away. Can the kids play together?" We saw bare flashes of each other those early years—running away from home, leaving the plastic shopping bag of bottles and instructions. Finally, it was a routine: one afternoon off for me and one for Joanne.

Joanne's husband worked long hours at his store, and my husband traveled a good deal, so she and I began to get together once or twice a week for a dinner ritual which my tiny son learned to call, "Going to the joint." We picked the local pizza place because it served wine (we never dared ask what kind), and Joanne and I would guzzle questionable chablis as my son burned his mouth on pepperoni and Joanne's daughter begged to dance in the aisles to the jukebox. Once in a while one of us would take a deep breath and drive all four little children to the A&W in Daly City for dinner, watching them gargle root beer and praying that none of them would wet in the car on the way home. Our pleasure came from knowing that the neighbor mommy had some time at home, blissfully alone.

A friend of mine who had suffered a stillbirth some time ago asked her obstetrician if the tragedy could have been caused by some tensions and worries that she'd had during pregnancy. Perhaps to ease her mind, the doctor had scoffed at the idea and replied, "There's no time in this life when there isn't trouble."

His answer comes back to me as I look at the time that Joanne Miller and I shared a neighborhood block and a six-year chunk of each other's lives.

Had our inter-dependent relationship started with my son's hospitalization when he was 18 months old? When he was whisked to the hospital with convulsions, who else was I to call, frightened at the suggestion of meningitis, but Joanne to tell her to sidetrack houseguests who were to arrive any moment. Who else but Joanne was I to ask to feed our concerned older child and reassure her that her little brother would be okay. (And he was okay. He was home in another day, with a diagnosis of bad tonsils and no more.)

Joanne herself took a trip to the hospital several months later to have a lump removed from the side of her neck. The surgery was to be routine, but it turned out to be otherwise. Joanne whispered the grim words to me as we walked up quiet hospital halls: "Malignant," she said, her normally cool brown eyes filled with tears.

I went home and shouted at my husband that it wasn't fair and threw something—a book? a pot?—at the wall so that my daughter came down alarmed and asked what was wrong.

But even the events of those frightful months that followed Joanne's initial surgery are faded now. Thyroid cancer has a good recovery rate, and Joanne's diseased gland was removed. I do remember all the children, certainly most of all her own, being frightened when she went to the hospital for the second time. But I remember them laughing, too, when she came home enclosed in a white bandage around her neck that made her look like a bride in a high-necked gown.

Was it the next summer that my back went out the night the Miller children slept over? I remember being frozen like one of those cartoon characters after someone has poured concrete over him, and Joanne had to come rescue me and maneuver my pain-racked body to the bed. Yes, that was three years ago. It was also the summer that my daughter accidentally kicked out the four-year-old Miller kid's two front teeth. Joanne joked that it was her way of getting even for the broken arm that my daughter had suffered on the Miller jungle gym the summer before.

Two years ago, my husband had to have his gall bladder out, and the Miller kids were the first to line up ("I feel like a freak show," my husband scowled) to see the incision when he returned home.

None of us was prepared for the most recent trouble to hit our home. Last summer my husband suffered a mild heart attack and was in the hospital for weeks.

Of course, I sometimes ponder what I would have done without the Millers in this soap-opera-like series of events. How many hours have our kids spent at their house? At their table? Being listened to by different, and sometimes more sympathetic, ears? Perhaps Joanne Miller wonders the same thing, although she has more family around the area than I do. The closest relative I have is a 65-year-old aunt in Los Angeles.

My sisters did call when my husband lay in the Coronary Care Unit. "Wish we could *do* something," they said sincerely through the crackle of the long distance line.

"That's okay," I told them. "I've got good neighbors."

I knew that the Millers would eventually move. Joanne had complained about her tiny house ever since I met her, and this year she informed me that she and her husband were looking in earnest for a larger house in Marin County. Every Sunday, after their trip across the Golden Gate Bridge and back, I would call them and ask apprehensively, "Found anything?"

Finally the answer was yes.

The news hit me hard when my daughter brought home a sack of end-of-school junk in June and out fell one of those little school photos. It was of the Miller's younger daughter, grinning with the first grader's mischief. Was this the same child that I had seen six years earlier in her mother's arms, head bobbing uncertainly, her infant mouth shaping the same grin?

I sobbed as I looked at the photo, for I knew that I was, in some way, losing one of my own. My daughter, now almost nine and very wise, said, "That's okay, Mommy. We'll see them again." But she isn't wise enough to know that while we will probably visit them once or twice, or a half-dozen times, eventually our separate realities will narrow us down to an obligatory name on a Christmas card list.

The photo will most likely be placed in our family album. Years from now my daughter, grown up and out of our house, will glance at the picture and ask, "Who is that cute little girl?"

# Getting to Headcheese: City People Butcher Their First Pig

*by Jerrold Mundis*

Saturday, toward the end of March, was sunny, and the sky was light blue with a few rills of cloud. The temperature was in the 50s, comfortable for a sweatshirt. The grass was beginning to green in patches, clipped forsythia branches had bloomed indoors, and the sugar maples were filling Charlie's sap buckets for the second time.

Charlie is a photographer who works three days a week in Manhattan, but lives up here with his wife and children in a barn he's renovating. He'd told me the day before that he and two friends had bought a pig and were going to butcher it Saturday: the economic crunch tightens, and necessity becomes the mother of necessity. He'd asked if I wanted to help, or watch.

Early Saturday I drove over to Jim's house—Jim was one of Charlie's partners—to see how things were going.

There were five men in the yard, and a 225-pound pig. The pig was lying on its side behind Jim's van, his legs trussed. It hadn't been stuck yet. Picking it up at the farm, where the van had become mired in mud, and preparing equipment had consumed the morning. The problem of the moment was that while the polyurethane hoisting rope was more than strong enough, it was hard to knot properly and the animal's shank bristles acted as a lubricant, causing the rope to slip from the legs. The pig's docility surprised me. It was lying calmly with its eyes open, breathing shallowly, a billow of white foam around its jaws; I learned later that this was a young animal that had never been out of its pen; its capture, tying and trans-

---

*This story is from* Harper's Weekly, *published from late 1974 to early 1976, which featured reader-written articles. At that time Jerrold Mundis lived in Ulster County, New York. Neither* Harper's Magazine *nor this editor knows where he is today.*

portation had sent it into shock. There was embarrassment and uneasiness about this, but also a certain gratitude: because its responses were depressed, the pig was being spared active terror.

We were quietly rational as we worked with the block, the rope, the webbing and the clamps, and stoked the fire that was heating water in an oil drum. Beneath that, though, was a palpable underlay of tension. We were all city people, only two or three years removed to the mountains. If any of our collective forebearers had ever slaughtered their meat with their own hands, they were a generation or two gone, and their experience and knowledge were lost to us. Our sobriety was marked. We were dealing with blood. It subdued us and made us apprehensive, and we protected ourselves with the meticulous application of logic.

We tried to raise the pig once more, but the rope slipped off one of its legs again as the hindquarters began to lift. So we lowered it back, disgusted and ashamed, because this was our third attempt and though we were ready to kill the beast we were not willing to abuse or torment it.

It would be stuck on the ground, then.

We rolled it to its back and it didn't resist. With nothing said, Jim drew a hollow-ground hunting knife from its sheath and went to stand at the pig's snout. There had been no previous discussion of who would do the killing. If the slaughter had taken place on Charlie's land, I think he would have picked up the knife. But this was Jim's province. Still without words, Charlie assumed the role of next importance. He straddled the pig's chest, bent and took hold of the forelegs. The rest of us variously gripped the hindlegs or hunkered beside the shoulders to help Charlie. David, an actor who lives in the country when he is between roles, walked several paces away.

Jim positioned the knife an inch lower than the midpoint between the base of the pig's jaws. He was intent and careful. He paused a fractional moment, fingers tight around the handle, then pushed the blade in. It penetrated four inches, to the guard. The pig twitched, but that was all. It neither struggled, nor made a sound; there was no well of blood. Now Jim had to cut down toward the breastbone—the jugular was in there somewhere. He pressed the blade forward, drew it out half its length, then pushed down again, a kind of slow saw, the white flesh and thick fat parting as easily and cleanly as a press of courtiers before their lord, the blood flowing now, dark crimson, the cut opening into what looked like a lightless cave, the final three-inch wound resembling nothing so much, at the first moments, before the blood filled it, as the vagina of a young girl.

The pig screamed, a shrill, high shriek that set dogs barking a quarter of a mile away.

The bleeding became profuse, flooding, and the pig began to thrash. A hind leg pulled free and the sharp hoof nearly struck Charlie in the groin before we could grab it again. The animal stilled, lay quietly a minute or two, squealed and resisted briefly a second time, then appeared to lapse into a coma. It emerged twice, once to jerk weakly and once to lap its own pooling blood, then did not move again. Gradually the blood flow lessened. And the animal died. It had taken about eight minutes in all. The paucity of its resistance had been startling. We were relieved; it became clear why, in other times, so much importance had been attached to the consent of the sacrifice.

Jim cleaned his knife. We looked down at the pig and we were all, I think, unsettled by the vulnerability of our own lives; like the carcass before us with its legs in the air, we were simply meat hung on a skeleton and bagged in skin.

David walked back. "It was strange," he said. "You were all looking someplace else, not at the pig, and not at each other."

This time we managed to knot the rope so it held. The block was fixed to the limb of an ash tree 12 feet above. We were taken aback by the effort required to hoist 225 pounds of dead weight—we are all in our 30s, healthy and of reasonable strength, but we had to strain to our limits. We secured the end of the rope around another tree, rigged a second to the pig and then ran it through the pulley and down to the bumper of a car, which would make future raisings and lowerings easier. Then we freed the first rope and tied it around the forelegs to use later as a guideline.

The women appeared about this time: Charlie's wife Nan with her infant daughter; Jim's wife with their 2½-year-old son; Stan's wife (Stan, an art director, was one of the partners);

David's wife; and Harold's girlfriend (Harold is a Danish photographer who'd had some experience sectioning meat). All but Jim's wife were formerly city women. There was less a sense of husbands and wives than of mates and allies. They looked curiously at the pig and asked questions about the sticking.

We had talked of catching the blood in a pot for blood sausage, but that would have been too awkward with the pig on its back. As much as a quart had run into the jowls. We could have opened them now and jugged it, but no one wanted to any longer, so we let it go.

Someone jokingly called Jim a killer. He resented it.

We put a thermometer into the heating water. It was 160 degrees, hot enough for scalding. Jim threw a couple of cans of wood ash into the water, which would help soften the bristles. We had a problem of logistics. The oil drum, which, carefully, had only been filled halfway—so that the volume of the pig, when it was immersed, would not cause an overflow—was about seven feet from where the carcass was hanging. We couldn't just lower the pig into it, but had to ease it down at a severe angle. The drum mouth was only two feet in diameter and we were worried about the carcass' weight coming to bear on the side and tipping the drum over. Four of us took the guide rope while Jim and Harold grasped the pig. Jim's wife got in the car and slowly began backing, lowering the pig while we struggled to align it vertically over the drum. Once again there was a burgeoning sense of community and mutual concern as the pig's head and shoulders went in, but its chest pressed against the drum side with increasing weight. The drum unbalanced.

"Get away!" Stan yelled to Jim and Harold. "It's going over!"

Jim grabbed the edge of the drum, which was hot, and leaned against it and shouted, "No, keep going!" and Harold shoved against the pig's loins and we lowered the carcass rapidly; if the drum went, 30 gallons of scalding water would go sloshing over Jim and Harold. But we did it. Great clouds of steam rose from the drum, a little water lapped the rim and stung Jim's fingers, and we all stepped back. There were smiles and a visible loosening of tensed shoulders.

The hind legs and the top of the hams protruded from the

water. We doused these with a ladle. No one knew precisely how long the pig should remain there; too little time and the bristles wouldn't be ready to shave, too much and the pig would start to cook. We tested by scraping a ham with a knife. When we could shave the bristles easily we took the carcass out, about three or four minutes. We lowered it onto a clean tarp and cut slits between the bone and tendon just above the first joint of the hind legs. We set the hooks of a weathered old gambrel holding the legs spread open.

There are special scrapers for removing bristles, as there is a special slaughtering knife with a hooked tip that one inserts and twists to sever the jugular—if experienced or lucky enough—but we didn't have these and so we shaved the carcass clean with knives, women and men taking turns. The ears, the areas around the hooves, and the tail were the most troublesome, having no flat planes. When we ran into a resistant patch we ladled more hot water on, and that eliminated the problem.

The white bristles clumped on the tarp and someone asked, "Isn't there a use for pig bristles?" and two or three others answered that quality paint brushes and shaving brushes were made with them, but no one knew how to do that, so with a little reluctance we washed the bristles away with a hose. Harold was using a thin boning knife. He grew fascinated with the shaving and was pleased that he didn't nick the skin even slightly. He said, "I've wanted to get a straight razor, but I've been afraid. Now I think I can handle it."

Jim brought out an issue of *Mother Earth News* with an illustrated article on pig butchering excerpted from a Morton salt manual. First step was decapitation. Following the instructions Jim read, I knelt and grasped the ears with downward pressure. Harold cut the throat. Our hands became bloodied (the only step in which they did) as the stuff trapped in the jowls drained out. From the front, Harold struck the neckbone a severing blow. Blood spattered onto my face and glasses, and the head came off in my hands. We washed it clean and Jim's wife took it away.

Harold handed his knife to Jim. "You do the rest," he said. "This is making me sick." He walked off.

The gutting consumed an hour. A professional probably

could have done it in seven or eight minutes, but we were being slow and careful, with David reading the instructions aloud—lapsing occasionally into stylized elocution or an interpretation based on a character that popped into his mind—and we stopped at intervals to compare our progress with the photographs.

Charlie and Jim did most of this work, sleeves rolled up, their arms thrust into the abdominal and chest cavities to their elbows, their skin becoming greasy and the knife handles growing slippery.

David stroked his jaw and looked contemplatively into the opened abdomen. He shook his head sadly. "It's hopeless," he said. "Close him up."

"There must be *something* we can do with the ears."

"Turn them into silk purses."

Cars passed by on the road while we were working on the suspended carcass. Most slowed appreciably and no one in them failed to stare at us. Some honked and waved. A few gave us looks of disgust. A Manhattan man and his wife with four children pulled over and watched for 10 minutes.

We separated the liver, lungs and heart from the pile of organs on the tarp and washed them off. They would be eaten too. There was an aesthetic satisfaction in their healthiness. A couple of us considered feeding the remaining offal to our dogs (the filled guts of graze animals are highly nutritional, and in a wild state canines will tear open the belly of game they have killed and eat them first), but we fretted about trichinosis and none of the sourcebooks we had at hand could clear the issue, so we let it go and buried the stuff.

As we washed down the inside of the carcass someone said, "A few hours ago, this was a living, happy animal."

"What you say," someone else answered in annoyance, "is that it's only a carcass now, but before long it's going to be chops and roasts and bacon in the freezer."

Harold could have given us the tour, but he wasn't around, so we examined the pig and speculated on just what part was what, and I think we were pretty accurate, and we were pleased with our deductions, and our only disagreement revolved about just where the short ribs were.

Charlie took a cleaver and with short, aimed chops split

the backbone perfectly from the hindquarters down, halving the pig except for a couple inches of flesh at the neck, which provided a joined splay, the optimum condition for allowing the carcass to cool. It would hang overnight in a temperature that would drop to the 30s, and Harold would reduce it to butcher's cuts. Jim brought out a jug of wine.

There's something disturbing in this kind of slaughter. It's not impersonal, as a gunshot is; or ameliorated by the predacious instincts of the hunter; nor the urgent and sanctioned spilling of blood in combat. It's a kind of murder, and two or three years ago it would have been beyond the perimeters of any of our lives. But we'd done it this afternoon, discovering a capacity about which none of us had been entirely confident, and done it well.

When I went into Jim's house at the end of the day to wash the last of the dried blood from my hands, I saw a large pot of water simmering on the stove. Onions and carrots floated on the top, above the pig's head. I don't like headcheese, but I was glad that someone did.

# Of Poetry, Dust and Death

*by Christopher Biffle*

*February 1975*

Last September I took a leave of absence from my job as a junior college philosophy instructor. I was sick of thinking and living only inside my head. I lived in a world that was so frustrating, so cerebral and so uncertain I felt as if my senses were wrapped in cotton; I could feel nothing hard, clear, cold, nothing straightforward and nothing I could take any clear action against.

To counterbalance this mental life and this uncertainty, I joined Cesar Chavez's United Farm Worker's Union as a photographer and reporter for their newspaper, *El Malcriado*.

In six manic weeks I had the opportunity, which I avoided, to be badly beaten 11 times. I saw death and could not move or speak. At twilight, 10 miles south of Stockton, in dust 6 inches deep, I saw poetry, which has for 12 years been my secret labor, really working. Finally, in Livingston, California, I was with history when it was taking place.

Six weeks—but I feel as if I have seen it all. And like a world weary Candide, I have retired. My lessons do not remain with me as axioms; I could not write them down as a list. What is left with me is perhaps five images, one terrible cry of grief and a feeling of intense, suffocating heat.

While I worked for the union newspaper, there were wildcat strikes going off all over the state; I was sent to most of them. They all took place on the same stage—the vast, green plain that runs through the center of California. Bakersfield, Fresno, Merced, Stockton, Delano, Sacramento, Highway 99—a monumental flatness. And everywhere for hundreds of miles there seems to be nothing but chalkline-straight rows that fan

---

*Christopher Biffle teaches philosophy at San Bernadino Valley College in California.*

unendingly past the car. A country of tomatoes. A nation of lettuce. An entire universe of grapes.

The framework of my experience was dust.

It was a strange passage, going from the sanitized world of the teacher into a place where dust was almost entirely and absolutely the center of things.

Dust seems to be half a foot deep all over Central California in the summer. After the first hour of the morning you feel gritty all over. Your pockets and boots and hair and ears fill with it. You can feel it between your teeth and when you lick your lips you can taste it. Everywhere you sweat it turns into a film. You can't avoid breathing it; by the end of the day it seems to have gotten entirely inside you, deeper than your skin, and you are possessed by it.

I have seen dust so deep in places that cars sank to the axles in it. In Indio, I saw four men who needed a fifth to move a Vega.

Once 15 men, 10 of them shouting different things in Spanish, pushed my old union Valiant 25 yards while I spun the wheels and dust fumed over everything before the car would move on its own. Dust this deep is worse than snow or mud; one is not prepared for it and can never tell where on the road it will be bottomless.

Incredibly, at one point early in my experience in the union I became so dust filled and so hot I now believe my entire sense of things was transformed. Near Coachella in Southern California, I decided I needed a picture of some strikers out near the grape vineyards. The men at the union headquarters were happy to have their pictures taken and we had soon filled six or seven cars. They told me they knew a good place, in the middle of some fields where there would be no trouble, but that it was a little hard to get to.

In five minutes we had left the main road and were driving down two dirt ruts with vines close to the car on both sides.

Each car dragged a huge balloon of dust behind it. I was about the middle car and the dust was thicker than fog. For long moments the car in front disappeared and I could barely see the vines on either side.

Of course, I immediately rolled up the windows. And then the car was, in that trite but very accurate phrase, like an oven. It was as if the sun was in the car.

Sweat was bursting through my skin and then out through my clothes; my shirt and pants were drenched and I could feel the sweat wrung out of my hair and leaking into the corners of my mouth. It tasted like tears.

The car was bouncing in and out of the ruts as I tried to go as fast as I could. The steering wheel was so hot I could not put my fingers around it; I guided the car with the heels of my palms. It was like being sealed in a can and then thrown into a fire.

Even though I had closed the windows, the dust still filled the car. I could see it hanging suspended in the air between my face and the windshield. Silent and motionless in the perfect heat, it was in strange contrast to the dust that furiously foamed over the hood outside. I was carrying this small and stable compartment of dust through a billowing ocean of dust. Dust powdered everything inside the car, the dashboard, the seat, my clothes, and it was soon so thick that I was afraid I wouldn't be able to use my camera when I arrived.

I was so hot and drowned in dust that I couldn't think. I have this final image of myself, no longer "a philosophy teacher," hundreds of miles from all the mysteries and uncertainties of students and teaching, hunched over the wheel, sweating from every pore, trying to see through the still dust inside the car and then beyond through the dust that was billowing across the hood, the sweat rising in little bubbles even on the backs of my fingers and leaking down into my eyes, in that terrible, baking stillness. Inside the car I felt that undeniably and unquestionably, I had found the real world.

About the third week I worked for the United Farm Workers, I was sent to Bakersfield to cover the funeral of a young union member who had been shot to death by the police. Apparently there had been a party, the police had been called, there was rock throwing and somehow, in the course of this, the youth was shot several times by an officer.

When I arrived, a large, entirely silent crowd was standing outside the church. It was early morning but there was no wind and it was already hot. After a few moments, people began to come out of the church followed by six men carrying a large silver coffin. The crowd formed in a long line behind them in the street and they began to walk to the cemetery.

For some reason, I became fascinated by the problem they had carrying the coffin. The men were using folded pieces of towel as cushions on their shoulders and after three blocks they had all begun to sweat heavily. The coffin was so large and expensive they could find no way to carry it easily.

Six or eight men walked behind the coffin. Every 30 or 40 paces, one of the men carrying the coffin had to be replaced. There was no easy or smooth way to do this and no way at all to do it without stopping completely. The coffin would be lifted and slightly tilted so that the men who had tired could get out from under it and then it would be very awkwardly held while his replacement got underneath and adjusted the towel on his shoulder.

Each of these complete stops moved back through the line like a ripple. There were so many people that the leaders had already started before their half reached those at the end.

As they went further, and as it got hotter, each man had to be replaced at shorter intervals. Some of the men ran forward and directed traffic so that they could walk through red lights, but there was no real way to make it easier. The men were not used to carrying a coffin. They did not know how to walk smoothly in step, and the farther they went, the more awkwardly they walked.

The crowd behind them was patient. Each time they had to halt, everyone quietly came to a stop. The men had a long way to go in this stuttering way, but there was really nothing else they could do.

When they reached the cemetery, they carried the coffin in under a large canopy that was open on four sides. They rested the coffin on several broad straps that stretched across the grave.

A large crowd gathered on the grass. Someone had brought large tubs of water and people stood quietly drinking out of white styrofoam cups.

I saw the family for the first time under the canopy. I assumed the younger children were the boy's brothers and sisters or perhaps cousins. His mother, who was seated, wore a black mantilla. She was holding a white, delicate handkerchief against her mouth and was pressing her head against the side of a man standing next to her.

I was standing in the second rank of the crowd around the canopy taking pictures. A priest stepped forward and stood at the end of the grave and opened his Bible. Everyone was quiet. The boy's mother was weeping silently.

Then something happened that was terrible and entirely natural yet shocking. The boy's mother threw her head back and let out a single awful scream. It was so loud everyone looked immediately at her. Then she curled over and began to weep helplessly. Her first cry of grief was so harsh and dry that it must have burned in her throat. I saw all this through the camera, but I could not move; as soon as she shrieked, I could feel the tears start in my eyes.

There was so much in that single terrible noise that I can hardly describe it. I had been occupied that whole day taking pictures, trying to keep up with the line and watching the way the men were having a hard time with the coffin. The crowd around the tent had been silent, and the silence was heavier because there were so many people. The priest was just beginning to read in solemn tones. It was a moment when one could hardly have coughed without embarrassment. Then she shrieked and it was very long and raw, high pitched, letting out her entire broken heart; helplessly and without restraint. I felt as if I had been suddenly snapped awake out of the life I had led, even the life I had led through that day with the camera—what was I doing there and worse, what was I doing there taking pictures? I continued taking pictures even as I thought this, but finally, for long moments, I could not bring the camera to my face and then I could not do it at all. The boy's mother was so ravaged by her grief I was embarrassed to even continue witnessing it but could not move enough to turn away. My eyes stayed open and I saw death as a brilliant and terrible fact, simple and obscene and without remedy.

I encountered poetry in a very unlikely place. One night south of Stockton there was a large rally; Manuel Chavez, Cesar's brother, had just finished speaking. A professor who had come up from Mexico told Manuel that he would like to say "a few words to the crowd."

The professor was a large man, big nosed, ample bellied, with a face that could never be called handsome but that was so rough molded it might, in certain lights, be interesting, even distinguished. He was also, it turned out, the wildest and most exciting speaker I had ever heard.

He spoke in Spanish and said he was a little afraid. Some in the crowd called to him not to be afraid. They addressed him jocularly, calling him Professor. He said in a round and rich voice that he was a simple man and no speaker and could only say what was in his heart and had no fancy words or turns of phrases—and he said all this in the way that a fine speaker will deny his ability and in the very manner he denies it, prove it.

He began to speak of the farm workers' *hambra para justicia*—their hunger for justice. The more he talked, the looser he became, falling down in a whisper across certain powerful phrases, letting his voice crack in anger at others, shaking his fist, rolling his head back and forth.

How would the ranchers like to feed their children as we, the poor people of the earth, must feed our children? How would they like to sit down at our table? The day will come when they will be on their knees grinding corn, grinding corn for whom, you ask me this, brothers and sisters? For us!

And all the time he was gaining in energy, shaking his large angry head, waving his arms, and the crowd began to grow in excitement. They interrupted or punctuated his speech with cries of *Yes! That is so! You are right, Professor! That is how it is done!* All of these phrases sounded sweeter and more natural and excited in Spanish. And then he suddenly stopped. We were all transfixed. The sun had set, we could just barely see each other and he said quietly he would like to recite a little poem that he knew. With our permission, of course; he did not want to keep us too long.

I believe then we all sensed that he had planned this, his speech, the phrases, maybe even this dramatic pause, the request for a few additional moments, the concluding poem, but if we all understood that it was a speech of more craft and forethought than it had appeared, we loved it entirely. Yes, of course! Let us hear the poem!

Incredibly, the poem was by Victor Hugo. It was about the French Revolution and he gave the kind of introduction I would have felt comfortable with in a college classroom. But

I was amazed, being a teacher, that everyone listened though many knew little about the French Revolution, much less Victor Hugo. I really knew nothing about him myself. But the professor had brought us to a state where we would have eagerly listened to him read to us from the telephone directory.

I was exhilarated. Here was learning, out of the ivory tower, down in the dust, going straight into the hearts of honest and simple people. Amazing! Suddenly there seemed no distance at all between the university and the fields.

And the poem began, highly musical and rhythmic and immediately emotional, and very sad. It was about a little "rubio," a blonde-haired boy who had no food. The soldiers beat him and laughed cruelly, and then the revolution came and here he was with his little friends on the barricade and the troops were coming and he did this and shouted that and addressed his comrades encouragingly and he was shot and began to speak his last words to his parents. The professor's voice kept reaching crescendos and then falling away into near tears, choking out some words, the poem nearly rasping in his throat in his fury, almost growling at times, his eyes filling with glistening tears as the boy was shot and some of the crowd began to weep and some cried *Que viva el professor! Que viva Victor Hugo!* Some laughed a little, made nervous by the intensity of the emotion, but most were stunned and deeply moved, totally unprepared to be brought to tears by a Frenchman who wrote a poem about a struggle that was 280 years old. And none was more moved or choked than I.

I had been grinding my bones away for 12 years writing poetry, isolated, unread, hours of unending effort, constantly conscious that it was, I thought, for the few and would never be read perhaps even by them and was generally of little or no use. But here it was in an undreamed of place, speaking right to people, speaking in terms they admired and loved but could never themselves make. I cried and at the same time wondered if I could ever write about it.

But the professor kept going. Our tears dried, the "rubio" was forgotten, other characters entered and left, his crescendos began to be predictable. It was now totally dark and he began, impossibly, to seem a bit boring, a bit overly dramatic. He rolled on and on. He had had us, had crushed our hearts until we couldn't bear anymore and then he wouldn't stop. The poem wouldn't finish. We shifted our feet, we lost interest, we looked at the stars, we scratched. Well! He was an academic after all. The ultimate and finest pleasure was in speaking, not in being heard. Finally it was over, we were raw inside from too much feeling and then from not being released and we felt cheated and used.

But still we had seen something, some of us, and I perhaps most of all. The professor stepped off the stand, was embraced by several men, slapped on the back, a straw hat put on his head and then, in fun, pushed down over his eyes.

I fell in love with two lady carpenters I met in Stockton. I didn't know them long enough to separate them in my feelings; I loved them together, as a unit.

One was fair and one was dark. I had met them both in Delano, where they were working on a retirement village for Filipino farm workers but nothing, or very little, had passed between us.

There was a huge strike in tomatoes in Stockton and everybody in the union, from clerks on up, had been sent there because it was rumored there was going to be a confrontation with the National Guard.

I met a lot of people I had seen briefly before, but since we were all so far from our usual work and since our situation there seemed so potentially exciting, we invariably greeted each other as ancient comrades.

I met the two women in a motel parking lot; somehow I had managed to get into one of the few rooms available to union people. They had been sleeping for the last several nights in one of several open-sided tents set up for people the union couldn't afford to rent a room for.

I felt happy to see them, for some reason happier than I would have expected to be. They both looked very tired, and they hadn't been able to bathe in several days. They wanted to know if they could use the shower in my room. I went up to the room, let them in, and told them I wouldn't be back for several hours.

The next time I saw them was the following night. I had had a frustrating afternoon waiting hour upon hour to speak for five minutes with one of the strike leaders who had endless streams of people seeing him. They had been through something similar earlier that day with the same person. Since then, they had gotten depressed and homesick. They walked toward me across the dark motel lot, the dark one comforting the fair, and seeing me they both smiled. One said, "Well! Let's sit down here and talk to a real person." And we talked for a while.

The next day I was suddenly given a new assignment. It was arranged that I should leave Stockton by driving a huge Avis van back to Los Angeles. I was happy to be going, but I still felt like a pawn and was really too tired to be excited. The normal day for everyone had been running 15 to 18 hours for several weeks.

Just as I was about to leave, I saw them in the rear view mirror. I called to them and they stepped up on the running board of the truck. I put my hands out to them across the seat and they reached their brown, slim arms in through the window and we looked at each other, squeezing each other's hands, and had a perfect tired communion. We were all so worn out that we were totally open and without frivolity or formality. We said good-bye gently. I told them I cared for no one else in Stockton so much as I cared for them. It caused me no difficulty at all to say this and caused them no uneasiness to hear it. I took my hands slowly out of theirs, they stepped back off the running board, I put the truck in gear, looked at them and backed the truck onto the highway.

The last thing I have to tell about happened in Livingston, California, which is about 10 miles north of Merced. I had been assigned to cover a small, unsuccessful strike there, and each day I went with the strikers out to the fields. The last day I was there seemed as if it would be, more or less, like the rest.

We had come out to an older vineyard where the grape rows were six and seven feet high and even though we were standing on a canal embankment above them we couldn't see whether or not there were even any workers in the field. We began chanting, "Huelga! Huelga! Strike! Strike!"

It seemed as if we were calling out to the grapes themselves. We couldn't see a single worker. We could have been at a field that wasn't being picked that day; there could have been 50 to 100 men and women down in the rows, clipping grapes, not 25 yards from us. We beat our hands and waved our banners and chanted hoarsely.

Then, way back in the field, we saw two men climb up on a tractor. We could just barely see them, but this gave us an object. The entire group, perhaps 100, began screaming "Huelga! Huelga!" A bullhorn was brought out, we delivered our entire energy to two men whom we had no way of telling could even hear us. One and then the other took off his shirt. They waved them over their heads and then, after awhile, they disappeared.

I have thought a lot about these two men. There was no way to read their expressions. The final image which colors and changes everything else is these two men in the distance slowly waving their shirts over their heads in mockery, or comradeship, or simple boredom.

# Silent Thunder in the Brain

*by Nancy Datan*

I want to talk about disturbances of consciousness, primeval disturbances of consciousness, interruptions in the brain's transactions. My friends take to drink or drugs to bring this about: as for myself, it is all I can do to stay cold sober. I marvel at them and envy them, but in my own brain cells transmissions occur. I have a scar on my head matched by one inside; somewhere on the cerebral cortex there is a glial scar which, interestingly, is not itself the focus of epileptic spike waves: my reading informs me that it is the relatively normal but damaged tissue surrounding the scar which discharges abnormally. I cannot help being fascinated by this peculiarity of my head: those who make a living by their wits are especially vulnerable—but I expect everyone is vulnerable—to injuries to the seat of consciousness.

If I wanted to pursue the matter in hospitals, I could locate the scar. But I have always been frightened of neurologists, who are of one breed, telling me that the EEG irregularities are "minimal"—what does minimal mean if it is my own head?—and in the next breath telling me I must, must take my medicine or I might have a seizure at any time—they pause, for emphasis—even crossing the street. It was two years after I first heard that warning before I could cross a street calmly. That is a lie. I am still frightened. Neurologists know their business and probably contribute to the combat effort in psychological warfare. Me they have conquered.

At any rate it is not a simple matter to extract information from neurology clinics.

Instead, I guess. The temporal lobes are most easily injured in a blow to the head; but I do not have olfactory hallucinations

*This story is from* Harper's Weekly, *published from late 1974 to early 1976, which featured reader-written articles. At that time Nancy Datan lived in Morgantown, West Virginia. Neither* Harper's Magazine *nor this editor knows where she is today.*

or disturbances of vision or any of the other symptoms a Chicago neurologist asked about, after pursuing the possibility of temporal-lobe epilepsy. The blow itself was delivered to the side of my head, high up on the left, and the external scar is painful to the touch today, five years later. "But that wouldn't localize the internal injury," the friendly Chicago neurologist, who had a gift for expression, told me, "because it isn't the blow which strikes the head—that's the *coup*—the brain itself is a kind of jelly anchored at the base, and when you strike the head the whole brain swings"—motioning with the hands—"and then swings back, hard, that's the *contre-coup*, which is usually what does the damage." Very interesting, doctor.

At the time I saw him, however, I was not in condition to appreciate his candor or his gestures. Yes, despite dire warnings I had reduced my medication—and who wouldn't, after all?—a deadline to meet and the paper blank in my typewriter and myself curled across three office chairs, asleep with the sun shining on my face. Nothing dire occurred at first: I wakened out of fog, the paper began to move along, colors grew brighter. I went shopping downtown.

I have since learned to appreciate the advance signals of color, and for this and other, related, reasons, my guesswork leads me to suspect a scar somewhere on the so-called "silent" areas—the associational cortex. At that time, however, I only saw colors beckoning to me; and as for the vertigo, I was determined to best it by an act of will. That is the whole secret of this disease: one would suppose a seizure to be heralded by drums and trumpets; but no, it is a silent thunder, all in the mind, until at last one falls, stricken by lightning, the tiny bolts of lightning of one's own neural synapses. No act of will can hold the thunderstorm at bay: the brain, the fountainhead of will, is vanquished by its own disorder: a built-in cure for arrogance.

Downtown, the colors fractionated; sensory perceptions fractionated. I had one last mission, in the store's basement, and riding the escalator I found myself going up. And then, overlaid on that discovery, a second: the escalator was going down. As it brought me into the basement I completed my imperfect train of thought: "My God, the down escalator I thought was going up was really going down," and with those triple layers of reasoning unintegrated, nevertheless managed to conclude, "My God, I must really be sick."

Reasoning might have prompted me to call home to ask for a ride, but I was beyond reasoning and made my own way home on public transportation, each step more difficult, conscious effort required to integrate the act of walking, relayed to me by my disintegrating consciousness as the pressure of my feet, one foot after the other, against the floor, the sidewalk, the street, the train; each door required several decisions: to acknowledge it, to raise my hand, to push it open, to walk through it, to close it or to allow it to close behind me. Traffic lights no longer magnetized me by their colors, but had begun instead to trouble my eyes, though I did not find it any easier to act on the cues: red, stop; green, go. A first-grade child would have done better. And crossing the street, I wanted things to cling to: stepping down off curbs and up onto curbs needed planning. The flashing lights of storefronts were past hurting and near to blinding me. Of course, as one of my colleagues remarked in a published paper, anyone can have a fit; it is merely a question of the level of the convulsive threshold: for most people the flashing lights tempt and excite. Others, myself, are too easily excited, too much. There is no boundary between us: only a question of degree. But I pursue consciousness with a fervor they give to the pursuit of intoxication. And sometimes I wish I could do as they do, as the whole world seems to do, and relax with a drink. I need one.

Home, finally, sicker and sicker. A friend with connections secured me a quick appointment in the University of Chicago's neurology clinic.

Background forms, a pencil. My name and address, which required some thought. The letters of the form, though, were very interesting, and the lines were becoming interesting too. Letters side by side, forming words, but more interestingly forming shapes, tailed by lines whose various lengths made interesting forms and shapes. Years of schooled diligence were not without their effect, and I filled out the forms, letter by curiously shaped letter, joining magically to make words. I had to think about spelling, which caused me to reflect that spelling was anyhow an arbitrary union of letters. Eidetic memory, a gift of the gods who also gave me a low seizure threshold to even things up, ensured accuracy of spelling, but did not inhibit the growing fascination with letters.

I was called, finally, weighed, measured and seated in an examining room. Presently a neurologist appeared, bearing my file with its fascinating letters, words, and lines. "Is it Miss or Mrs.— or Ms.?" he asked with a smile. Aha, sick, very sick indeed, but not dead yet: "It's Dr.," and I waited for the disbelief, in faded jeans and a tie-dyed T-shirt and my eyes mirroring the vacancy of others I had seen in the waiting room; surely I did not look capable of managing registration for courses, even.

"A Ph.D.?"

The letters struck my ears, familiar and friendly, without eliciting the obsession that letters in print had done. "Yes," thinking he was omniscient, failing to see that an M.D. would have had her own connections, and, moreover, would have known better than to despise the early warning signs of an aura. Though later I was to hear of a chief of neurology who died at 39 of intestinal cancer which he had persisted in treating himself, as an ulcer, when for an elevator ride he could have learned otherwise, had he been willing to trust his fellow-priests in internal medicine. I am not the only fool. If, that is, I am a fool at all, and not merely a frightened human being determined to make my own destiny.

"Well," recording the Ph.D., "you probably don't think much of our kind of science," amiably. And yesterday my associational processes wouldn't help me cross a street, but today they scent combat like a wolf pack: "I don't think science is defined by the five percent level of significance," I heard my own voice reply, "and I don't think psychology can be learned except by clinical studies." That statement, wherever it came from, required and consumed the last of my strength; and I submitted silently to neurological examination, learning that I was neurologically normal, apparently left-hemisphere dominant as most people are, though left-handed and, as the gesturing, swinging hands and the explanation of *contre-coup* indicated, probably scarred on the left hemisphere.

"How were you injured?" I had told lies about this for three years. I wasn't going to lie any longer. For one thing, I was not feeling very clever, and even at my desperate best I had had a difficult time inventing a plausible, innocuous source of injury; for another, the classical psychoanalytic interpretation of epilepsy, though pre-EEG and perhaps only 20th-century mysticism, spoke of a smouldering rage which erupted in convulsions. If telling the truth could save me, I would try it.

"My husband hit me." There. It was terrible enough to say, but certainly no worse than refusing liquor at friends' homes, saying "I don't drink" as he accepted his, needing it himself no doubt, but so did I; and finally, pressed by a longtime friend whose idea of humor it was to ask him, "What did you do to your wife that she doesn't drink?" interrupting the silence myself to say, "Alcohol gives me convulsive seizures," which was true in the subjunctive but not in the declarative mood: it would, if I dared drink; but since told I could not, I never dared. Psychoanalytic theory also teaches that humor is funny which perverts a painful truth.

I have, since, told people the truth at once, whenever they asked with any persistence; I learned that refusing alcohol was interpreted as indicative of alcoholism. Once I responded, "I don't drink but I make love a lot," which produced an agreeable sensation, and so I sometimes reused that as an alternate detour round interrogation. And our inquisitive friend, after all, must have had his own reasonable intuitions, for, though people have told me, "How awful," "How terrible," and even, "That's criminal," not one has ever said, "Gee, Nancy, I don't see why anyone would ever want to hit you."

"How?" taking notes, without expression.

"With a metal mug, he threw it, then he threw me against the wall, and my head must have struck the wall on the same spot because it didn't bleed from the first blow, but it bled all over after the second. The laceration looked to the doctor as though I had struck a corner, but I think it was a wall." Bled puddles all over the floor. I remember trying to mop up the blood myself.

"Did you lose consciousness?"

"I don't know." I opened my eyes to find myself covered with blood, perhaps I did, though I seem to remember everything, and I often dream of it even now.

"You're still married?"

"Yes." Too extraordinary an act to call the police, too terrible to be forgiven, the children were small and loved him very much. I was frightened. Also, concussed, and as they say, not in my right mind. But thinking it over in the years which followed, I was never sure what the best decision would have been. Soon after this conversation we would be divorced, though it was his decision, not mine; but perhaps I could understand that too, sometimes. Refusing responsibility for my medical expenses, denying any responsibility of his own. Well, one wouldn't want to admit it, I suppose.

"You have epilepsy, all right," briskly, the word is haunted. "We see this all the time in the clinic. It isn't the husband, of course," said too quickly, "but an automobile accident, usually. If you wanted to spend the money on an EEG, we could locate the site of the scar, but it's not really important—it's garden-variety post-traumatic epilepsy."

Garden-variety—I hated that, as though one's cortex might sprout dandelions.

Though later I learned that the metaphor reflected statistics faithfully enough, and perhaps one could do worse than dandelions, mowed down by the whirling blades of power cutters, seeding, springing back, ubiquitous, untameable, indestructible. "You might have killed her!" one doctor shouted at him, and I often wished he had, that the blow had been struck forward a little and down a little, at the weakest point of my skull instead of the strongest. Whoever said death before dishonor had to be thinking of firing squads, or of hangings: not of the little deaths I bought with silence, paid in installments, swallowed, 100 milligrams of death taken at bedtime, debts, fear, solitude: hanging is more convenient. But the lightning strikes and strikes again and, mindless as a dandelion, I survive. Garden-variety. Yes.

"With this kind of disturbance, most people don't have seizures at all, they just have auras," my friendly neurologist told me, prescribing drugs in a dosage which would have rendered seizures and ecstasy equally distant; surrendering, under protest, to my insistence on a single drug whose side effects I knew, probably able to surmise that he had merely been present at the latest, but not the last, of my battles against my own body's fallibility. "I'd feel safer if you'd take what I prescribed," he told me, but it is my safety, my mind, and I who must weigh them.

In the two years which have passed since then, the rhythm of defiance and submission has not altered, though the constant headaches of the very first years have abated, and I have grown more clever at anticipating my brain's treachery. When I err, it is out of the hope, which hasn't died, that the diagnosis was wrong or has expired; but I have not grown well, and I collapsed, to my surprise and his, against a colleague as we walked across a parking lot last week. If he was startled, he was kind; but this is the worst of diseases, legendary and terrible. I have seen eyes turn away from me as though I were possessed by a daimon or subject to visitation from God. And sympathy is no better, for it cannot be extended infinitely: the best diseases for sympathy are acute, intense, and soon over; next best, terminal diseases, which, after all, end; worst of all, chronic diseases, which are neither cured nor ended. This is a terminal disease taking an interminable length of time to finish me off: people will be sick of me, and I will still be alive and sick.

# Grandma Beely and the Shoe Store Sit-In

*by John Boe*

In 1953 when I was nine years old, we moved to Illinois. Since both of my parents were originally from the Midwest, this meant being near countless strange relatives. Without doubt the strangest one of all was my father's mother. Everyone called her "Beely" and she never knew or asked why. She just accepted it as her nickname, the way I accepted "Dobby" as my nickname. Actually the name Beely (which her own children had given her) was short for Beelzebub. Beelzebub is one of the Devil's names. That gives you a clue to the character of my Grandma Beely.

Whenever Grandma Beely came to visit we had to be careful not to leave any of our stuff on the floor. This was hard for us because we were normally a very messy family. But when Grandma Beely came to town, the floors were clean. You see, she liked to throw away things she found laying on the floor. She'd chirp with delight as she threw away toys, baseball cards, paper dolls, books, it didn't matter what. If you asked her why she'd thrown away your stuff, she'd simply say, "Order in the house is order in the world; the world is run by order."

Grandma Beely liked to snoop too. If she was left alone in the house she'd go through all the drawers, reading hidden mail and investigating bank books. Once one of my aunts put a note near the bottom of a drawer. It said, "Don't look any farther, Grandma." One afternoon when everyone else was out, Grandma came across that note. She was furious. "I've never been so insulted!" she exclaimed, "I was only looking for a pencil." We all knew better, but there was no arguing

---

*John Boe has been a construction worker, technical writer, nursery school aide, and fairy tale teller. Principally he's an "itinerant teacher," frequently of Jungian psychology and literature. Most recently he was a visiting lecturer teaching English composition at the University of California, Davis.*

with Grandma Beely.

Also, when Grandma Beely was around even things that weren't left laying on the floor were likely to disappear. We eventually discovered that Grandma Beely liked to steal things from one of her relatives and mail them as presents to other of her relatives. Before this was discovered, my sister Karen used to regularly get fine and fancy clothes in the mail from Grandma Beely. Grandma Beely explained that her grand-daughter Marie (who had closets full of fancy clothes) had outgrown these things. Finally one day my mother mentioned to Marie's mother how grateful Karen was for the clothes Marie had outgrown. "So that's what's been happening to all those things," Marie's mother said.

Given Grandma Beely's character, then, it is understandable that I was less than overjoyed at being told she was coming to visit for Easter. That meant being polite to her when she threw away my toys, listening to her constant jabber, and allowing her to call me John Jr. (which I hated). Oh well, it would only be for a week, and it really was hardest on my mother. She was the audience for most of Grandma's chatter. And she had to find good hiding places for those things she didn't want Grandma to find and mail away.

To further complicate things, I had to go shopping with my mother and sisters for new Easter outfits. I hated shopping trips, especially those involving my sisters. We went to various department stores, and my sisters tried on outfit after outfit, examined dresses, blouses, hats, shoes, petticoats and other items of girl's clothing. I alternately paced the floor or sat in one of those department store lounging chairs. I stared at the ceiling, I examined and reexamined my profile in three-way mirrors. Boring hour after hour I waited until finally my sisters had selected suitable outfits. Then, almost as an afterthought, we spent a few minutes picking out a "nice little suit" for me.

Just as we were finally escaping from Carson's Department Store, my mother murmured loudly to herself, "Shoes." "Dobby," she said, "you'll need a nice pair of shoes." I sighed and followed her back up the escalator to the shoe department. We quickly picked out a nice pair of black shoes that were "On Sale," and finally we left the department store for good. Or so I thought.

Grandma came and Easter came. "My how you've grown! My what beautiful blue eyes you have! And what do you want to be when you grow up, John Jr.? Ah, you are beautiful and smart just like all my grandchildren." I smiled at her chatter like a good grandson, but I wanted to say, "My how you've shrunk! What nice gray hair you have! But Grandma Beelzebub, I've never met your other grandchildren, and if that's what you meant by beautiful and smart, include me out." But I knew that if I said any of this, my mother would kill me, so I just smiled and submitted to her chatter and her kisses.

On Easter Sunday, we all got dressed up in our new outfits and went to church. After church we got Easter baskets, hunted for eggs, and got our pictures taken.

"Kids, come over here next to Grandma for a picture," my mother ordered. We went and stood where directed, and my mother snapped a picture.

"Dobby," she suddenly said, her voice a mix of question and anger, "what have you done to your new shoes?"

"Huh?" I responded with typical cleverness.

"Look at that shoe," my mother said, walking toward me.

I looked down, and sure enough my right shoe had a big rip in it. I took a step, and noticed that the sole flapped as I walked. The more I walked the more it flapped, till finally my new shoe began to make a smacking sound that I found rather amusing, clownlike.

Mother and Grandmother were not amused. I took off the offending shoe and handed it to them. They examined it with the seriousness of doctors deciding whether or not to operate. They finally concluded that no operations were possible, that the shoe was ruined. Then Grandma Beely decreed that "the shoes should be returned." My mother of course agreed, but she did allow as how the shoes had been worn all day, and that shoe stores usually wouldn't take back shoes once they had been worn outside. "Anyway," she added, "Carson's has a policy of no returns on sale items." Grandma Beely's tiny eyes lit up. Her small frame puffed up with the thought of a fight with a department store. "We'll return those shoes, won't we, John Jr.? We'll return them first thing tomorrow." I looked to my mother for help but she just shrugged. Grandma Beely stood there smiling at me as I squirmed. She acted like my squirms meant, "Oh yes, Grandma, I'd love to spend the first day of Easter vacation with you returning shoes." Somehow I couldn't explain that I never planned to wear these fancy shoes again anyway, that all I ever wore were gym shoes.

And so "Grandma Beely and John Jr." went off to Carson's early Monday morning. We put the shoes in the box they came in, although my mother had been worried that we didn't have the receipt. "Nonsense," Grandma Beely had said. "They'll know they're Carson's shoes. They'll be able to tell because of how they fell apart."

Grandma and I walked through the department store, up the escalator, and into the shoe department. We walked up to the man behind the counter.

"Can I help you? Shoes for the young man, perhaps?"

Grandma opened her eyes wide. "The problem is that we already bought the young man's shoes here. Show him, John Jr." I laid the box on the counter.

The smiling bald shoe salesman opened the box and examined the shoes. "I'm sorry, ma'm, but these shoes have been worn outside. We accept no returns if the shoes have been worn outside. Besides, I believe that these shoes were on sale for Easter, and we never accept returns on sale items. I'm sorry."

Grandma smiled politely. "But you see how the shoe has ripped."

The man picked up the torn shoe. "This shoe has obviously been abused. Boys will be boys, eh? Playing baseball in your new shoes, huh, son?"

Before I could answer Grandma answered for me. "These shoes were bought on Friday. They were only worn on Easter Sunday. To church. They don't play baseball in church, you know."

"Do you have the sales slip?" the salesman asked, wanting to change the subject from baseball in church.

"No, we don't have the sales slip."

"I'm sorry, then. It's impossible for three reasons to return these shoes." With that final statement the smiling bald shoe salesman turned his back and went to wait on another customer. Grandma stood patiently at the counter, and I stood with her. In about 15 minutes the man came back, rang up a sale, wrapped some shoes up, and then sent another customer happily on her way.

"I'd like to see the manager," Grandma demanded.

"I'm not sure when the manager will be in. And it won't do any good anyway."

"We'll wait."

"But he might not be in till late this afternoon. In fact he might not be in until tomorrow morning."

"We'll wait," Grandma said, and we sat down and waited. And waited. And waited. Department stores can be boring even when you're shopping, but they are triply boring when you are just sitting there waiting with your weird old grandmother. A few hours passed, then I said to Grandma, "I'm hungry."

"Oh goodness yes, it is time for lunch." She stood up and walked over to the smiling bald shoe salesman. "We're going to lunch now," she said. "We'll be back in an hour." The man stared at us blankly as we walked off.

We had hamburgers, fries, and cokes. I bought a baseball magazine and Grandma bought a newspaper. Then we went back to the shoe department to wait.

We sat and read and waited till mid-afternoon. "I've got to go to the bathroom," I said to Grandma. Grandma went up to our friend, the no longer smiling bald shoe salesman, and asked him where the bathrooms were. After the trip to the bathroom, I went back to my seat in the shoe department and reread my baseball magazine. Grandma just sat there, staring straight ahead. She seemed very sure of herself. I, on the other hand, was bored and nervous. I walked around the shoe department, looked at shoes, sat and read the newspaper, got up and got a drink of water, went to the bathroom again, sat down and started reading my baseball magazine still one more time. I even started a conversation with Grandma Beely. This was a mistake, for conversation with her consisted of her chirping out words faster than I wanted to understand them. So my mind wandered away, as Grandma rambled on about the need for order and neatness, about how dull nice people were, about how beautiful and smart her grandchildren were. I couldn't wait for 5:30 to come, for Carson's Department Store to close, for the chance to go home and really start my vacation.

Finally an announcement came over the PA system: "Carson's

is now closing. Thank you for shopping here." I started to stand up to leave, but Grandma quickly pulled me back down to my seat. Finally the smiling bald shoe salesman came over to us. "The store is closing now," he said. "I'm sorry the manager didn't get here, but he wouldn't be able to exchange the shoes anyway."

Grandma smiled up at him. "That's all right, we'll wait," she said.

"I'm sorry, you didn't understand, the store is closing."

"Oh yes, fine, we'll wait," Grandma chirped.

The man started to stammer, "But...but...the store..."

"Oh we'll be just fine here," Grandma reassured him. "We know where the bathroom is. We had a big lunch, and I have some crackers and candy in my purse. Don't you worry about us. You go on home, we'll just wait here."

The salesman stood there for a moment, and then he spoke slowly, clearly and loudly, as if he were talking to a foreigner, "The store is closing now." I felt dizzy and sick to my stomach at the idea of spending the night with Grandma Beely in the shoe department of Carson's Department Store. I knew that she was perfectly ready to spend the night there. In fact, she appeared to be looking forward to it.

Grandma gave the salesman a polite smile and then began reading the newspaper. The man cleared his throat and Grandma looked up. "I'm sorry," he said, "but you'll have to leave now."

Grandma smiled and stood up. "Certainly," she said, "but first we'd like to return this pair of shoes. I don't know if *you* can accept them for return. If not, we'll just wait for the manager. We can wait all week you know. John Jr. is on school vacation, and I really have nothing else to do. It's quite nice here."

The man merely moaned, "Ooohhh."

"If the manager can't accept them for return, then we'll just have to wait for the owner," Grandma said over the salesman's moan. I wondered who Grandma and I would wait for if the owner wouldn't accept them for return, but luckily things didn't get that far. The shoe salesman knew he was beaten. He went to the back of the store and returned with a brand new shoe box. He handed it to Grandma and Grandma handed it to me.

"Now please leave. Go home. I want to go home," the poor man said.

Grandma, in no hurry, looked him in the eye. "You'd better give us a sales slip, so we can return them if they break." As the man made up a sales slip, Grandma told me to try on the shoes. The man handed Grandma the sales slip and watched me putting on the shoes.

"How do they fit, John Jr.?" Grandma asked me.

"They fit just fine, Grandma," I said. I'd have said the same thing if they had fit like a glass slipper on one of Cinderella's stepsisters.

I started to take off the shoes and put on my sneakers, but Grandma Beely stopped me. "Wear them home, John Jr., wear them home. We have to make sure they don't break like that other pair." As we walked away the shoe salesman slumped over his counter and put his head in his hands.

No one ever walked as gently and carefully as I did. Fortunately the shoes didn't break on the way home, and we got home in time for dinner. Grandma told everyone the tale of her triumph, and my mother was impressed that we were able to return the shoes. I went upstairs and changed back into my sneakers.

Grandma stayed a few more days, and I didn't wear my new shoes even once. First of all, there was no need for me to wear fancy shoes, and second, I was scared to death of the shoes breaking again and my having to live in Carson's Department Store for the rest of the week. So the shiny new black shoes sat in my closet even though Grandma Beely asked me daily why I didn't wear them. When I'd say, "I'm saving them for special occasions," she'd say, "But it's special when your Grandma's here, isn't it, John Jr.?" I'd nod my head and give her a sickly smile, but I never went up and put on the new shoes.

Finally Grandma packed up to go stay with another of her children's families. She shuffled regularly around her five children's homes. Luckily we weren't her favorites so she never stayed very long with us. I dutifully kissed her good-bye, and my mother drove her off to the train station.

I didn't think of those shoes for several months until it was June and time for my sister's graduation from Junior High School.

"Put on your Easter outfit," my mother said, and so I dutifully put on jacket, tie and pants. But when I got downstairs my mother noticed that I was still wearing my sneakers. "Put on your good shoes, you know, the ones you got with Grandma Beely," she said. I went back upstairs and looked in the closet, but I couldn't find the shoes.

"I know I put them in the closet," I explained to my mother. "But they're just not there. I haven't worn them since I got them with Grandma Beely. I knew that if they broke Grandma would suddenly appear and drag me off to live in the shoe department." We all laughed, and then my mother said she'd go upstairs and find the shoes, that I looked for lost things just like my father did, without moving things about, looking under, around and beside. But the shoes were nowhere to be found.

"Well, I guess you can wear sneakers after all," my mother said wearily. "But I wonder what could have happened to those shoes?" Then my mother smiled at me and asked, "You say you haven't seen those shoes since Grandma Beely left?"

I nodded, then I realized what my mother was thinking and I smiled too. Grandma had taken my new shoes with her, to give as a gift to some one of my cousins.

"I just hope those shoes don't break again," my mother said. I looked at her, not understanding her concern. "I'm not sure," she went on, "that any of your cousins could survive living in a shoe department with Grandma Beely."